Prophets in the Sky

Prophets in the Sky

ALEXANDER PATTERSON

RESOURCE *Publications* · Eugene, Oregon

PROPHETS IN THE SKY

Resource Publications
An Imprint of Wipf and Stock Publishers
199 W. 8th Ave., Suite 3
Eugene, OR 97401

www.wipfandstock.com

PAPERBACK ISBN: 978-1-7252-8305-3
HARDCOVER ISBN: 978-1-7252-8306-0
EBOOK ISBN: 978-1-7252-8307-7

Manufactured in the U.S.A.   09/16/20

This book is dedicated to the parents and guardians of LGBTQIA+ children and to the children themselves, and to my own parents.

It is hard to stop seeing your son as a son and to start seeing him as a human being. It is hard to stop seeing your parents as parents and to start seeing them as human beings. It's a two-sided transition, and very few people manage it gracefully.

—DAVID LEVITHAN, *TWO BOYS KISSING.*

Contents

Acknowledgments

THIS BOOK COULD NOT have been written without the help of my writing and theology teachers, and the various parents of LGBTQIA+ children and clergy members I spoke with while researching the experiences of non-affirming parents. Professors Mark Olsen and Dr. Arna Bontemps Hemenway were both immensely helpful in shaping my writing and this story to being what it is today. All of my theology professors at Baylor University and Brite Divinity School have assisted in developing my theology through inquiry and empathy with those around them in the world and in the classroom. I am thankful to the members of Courage and Encourage, who met with me to talk about their experiences coming out and their experiences of being come out to.

Special thanks should also be given to the churches, organizations, and allies who help LGBTQIA+ youth who become homeless through their coming out process. No child should be driven from their home and those who assist these children in need deserve all the praise they can be given.

PART ONE

Wanted to Write a Love Song

Chapter 1

Lonely Moon

"THAT BITCH!"

"Mom!" Her boy's voice screeched over a riff of mellow ska trombones from the car radio, and a sudden honk from yet another day of insane after-school traffic. "You can't say that!"

"Sorry, sweetie." May turned from the line of cars edging toward the schoolyard's exit and flashed Chris an apologetic smile. Her son leaned against the passenger door, arms holding his raggedy backpack close to his chest. But he smiled back, pulling his lips wide and rolling his eyes. So maybe things would work out. "But she did cheat on you."

"Yeah," Ryan chipped in, scooting forward to nudge her brother; always eager to get in on the conversation even from the back seat of the car. "Lisa's a bitch."

"Language," May scolded, half turning to her daughter as she did. Ryan had her phone in hand; ready to bury her face back into the texts, Snapchat, Instagram, or whatever it was that kept her attention these days. The screen was off though, and her bright red hair had been pulled into a loose bun; something she only did whenever she was having a tough day. It was down most of the time.

"What?" Ryan's mouth hung open.

Chris shook his head, as if that could hide his smile. He couldn't mope about cheaters. Not if she had any say about it. He'd try, but she and Ryan would be there for him.

"Put a dollar in the jar when we get home."

"But Mom!" Ryan groaned theatrically and slid down against the car seat.

Mom. She would never stop loving the sound of that. May had worried that first year after Ryan's parents died that she would never hear that sound again. But now, Ryan's strong, curly Irish hair and freckled face were the only things that kept people from assuming they really were mother-daughter. Not like her and Chris.

"Hey, I'll be putting one in too, so stop your whining. And Chris, stop your pining."

Chris practically snorted at that. A huff of air like he wanted to laugh, but also wanted to look all mature and somber about everything. *Teenagers.* Couldn't be caught dead laughing at their mom's jokes, but he couldn't stop himself from smiling. Good. No way was Chris going to celebrate the last day of school by moping over a *huss*—over a girl who cheated on him.

The light ahead of them turned red, but May smiled as she brought the car to a stop. An ice cream truck—one of those new ones that sold gelato and sundaes and that didn't blare through neighborhoods with lights and bells—parked at the intersection's Exxon. Already, kids just out of school and adults alike formed a line that trailed from the truck to the station's door.

"How about we go there?" May asked. "Jar's almost full."

"Eh," Chris shook his head. "Scott says they're going to be doing a . . ." he tilted his head back in thought. "Summer-fun-in-the-sun-igloo-family-sundae-delight thing."

Ryan laughed. "When does Scott need to have the name by?"

"Mrs. Asim wants to start the deal on Monday."

Mrs. Asim made the best ice cream around, but she was terrible with branding. That left Scott, Mrs. Asim's only employee and Chris's best friend, to come up with all the names himself. The boy was good at it; had a future in marketing was what his mom always said. Elizabeth never said that around Scott of course. He didn't want to go into business. He wanted to be a musician, sing with symphonies, or tour with his favorite band: The Cat Empire.

And just as Elizabeth learned to not bring up business school in front of her son, May had learned to not bring up a performance degree with hers. The boy had talent, maybe not enough to become a world-famous musician, but enough to make a living. The one time she'd told Elizabeth this, her older friend had laughed and had said *spoken like a true millennial.*

"What's Scott thinking?" Ryan asked.

"Umm . . . he's between Eskimo's Delight and Brownie Town," Chris said.

May smiled. So, there were brownies in it. That was good. That was very good. "I like Eskimo's Delight."

"But Eskimos wouldn't eat ice cream," Chris pointed out.

The light turned green.

"How about Summer Fudging?"

"That's awful," Chris said, suppressing a smile.

May kept herself from rolling her eyes. Instead, she was content with looking in the rearview mirror at Ryan who didn't attempt to hide her laughter. Hopefully she'd never go through that phase of being embarrassed to have your parent tell a joke. She hadn't hit it yet; she might be in the clear on that one. If she hadn't developed it during her freshman year, she was probably never going to get it.

"Oh, come on. Pitch the idea to Scott. You're going to his gig tonight, right?"

"Please don't say 'gig,' Mom," Ryan said.

While Chris got embarrassed by May being funny, Ryan always got red-faced whenever her mom was cool. Figures.

"What? Come on, I'm still hip. I'm not forty yet; I can still say 'gig.'"

Ryan groaned and sank lower down in her seat. This time, Chris didn't hide his smile. He enjoyed seeing her mess with his little sister almost as much as he liked to do it himself.

"That's a no then," May half grumbled to herself. "What about ho-down? You are going to Scott's ho-down, right?"

Chris nodded, but said, "I'm still thinking about it."

He wanted to pout tonight, but God as her witness May was not going to let that happen.

"You should go. It's Maxine's last night isn't it?" Maxine was one of the brass players in the band. She was Scott's older sister and was moving north to attend law school.

"Yeah."

"It would be nice to see her off," May said. "Plus, it'll be good for you. Meet new people. Forget about *her* for a night."

"Have a rebound," Ryan added.

"Have a rebound. . ." May trailed off, realizing what she'd just told Chris to do. "No! I mean . . . like in a friend . . . sort of way." She sighed, which only caused Ryan to laugh more. She might as well commit to this joke of an error. "No, you know what? Make good choices, but, if you meet a girl . . ."

"Mom!" Chris was red-faced, but beneath his utter revulsion at hearing his mom encourage him to go out and have a rebound, Chris suppressed a smile.

"I know, sweetie. You'll behave, but you should go and put yourself out there. Maybe don't have a rebound." She glanced in the mirror to look at Ryan, who was glued to her phone. Neither of her kids would ever make the same mistakes she'd made. "But, try and meet some new people."

Heaven knew the boy could afford to.

May pulled into the driveway and glanced at the person kneeling in her garden. The woman's back was turned, but there was no mistaking her for anyone else. Elizabeth loved wearing those bright green and blue flannels whenever she gardened, along with that ridiculously large, broad-brimmed hat. Besides, no one else would be wrist-deep in May's garden—if it could even be called a garden. May never could get the hang of plants herself. She'd tried a few times, but they always died. Elizabeth kept telling her she just needed to commit to them, but May knew she didn't have a green thumb like her friend. Not that Elizabeth would give up on her though. They would try again this summer, but she didn't expect much. Chris opened the door and climbed out of the car.

"Hey, Mom?" Ryan asked. "Can I see a movie with Stacy tonight? We're gonna catch the end of the concert afterward."

"Is it that new superhero one?" May took her hand from the car door to face Ryan. They always seemed to be coming out with the superhero movies these days. And they were mostly good too. Not like the low-budget cash grabs she'd grown up with.

"Yeah. It starts at eight."

"Sure. Is Stacy driving?"

"Yee . . ." Ryan was buried back in her phone's screen. " . . . ees. Yeah." She looked up and nodded. "She says she can take me."

"Mom," Chris called from the front of the car. "Can you get the door?"

"Should we make him wait?" May asked.

"Nah, he's had a long day."

May opened the door as a means of response and tossed him her keys; he must have forgotten his own set somewhere. "Go on inside."

She walked toward Elizabeth, who leaned back to rest on her toes and wiped the dirt from her hands on her pant leg. The rows of bluebonnets they planted months ago were still alive, but they were not nearly as vibrant as those Elizabeth had in her own garden a few doors down. A pile of weeds and dead leaves lay in front of Elizabeth. Elizabeth had been busy in the ten minutes it took May to get the kids.

"How often have you been watering them?" Elizabeth asked.

"Once a day in the morning before taking them into school," May answered.

She nodded. "Use a little less water from now on."

She gestured for May to kneel beside her and poked around the dirt, showing her how the roots were engorged and weren't absorbing the water anymore. May was saved from further plant lecturing by Ryan.

"What's up, Mrs. Stracke?" she asked as she passed by.

"Oh, not much. We're just making sure these bluebonnets last past June this year."

"Cool." She glanced at her mother and blessedly changed the subject. "Hey, are you going to the concert tonight?"

"Oh, no. No, I'm too old to be out past midnight."

"I'll record a set for you," Ryan promised.

"Rock on." Elizabeth lifted her hand. Her middle and ring finger lay tucked beneath her thumb.

Ryan laughed and returned the gesture. "Catch you later."

May shook her head at her friend. "And not five minutes ago she said I was too old to say 'gig.'"

"Ooo," Elizabeth groaned. "You *are* too old to say 'gig.'"

"And you're not?"

"Oh, heavens no. *Rock on* is the limit of my lingo."

Elizabeth's phone buzzed, accompanied by a short bird whistle. She glanced at the screen. "Matt's landed. He's going to call once he gets a cab."

May nodded. Elizabeth's husband had left for a business trip to Toronto that afternoon.

Elizabeth pointed out where the flowers needed to be trimmed and instructed May to finish pulling the weeds.

May took her spot in the grass—for whatever reason weeds grew with ease all over her yard.

"Hey," she called out, "Why don't you come over for dinner tonight? We'll have the kitchen to ourselves and can make pasta."

Elizabeth smiled. "I'd like that. What time should I come over?"

May mentally walked through everything she had left to do. It turned out to not be much at all, just finish up the gardening, unload the dishwasher, and email her draft to the paper's Life Section editor.

"Seven?"

"See you then."

May returned to her work. She did the weeds first. Not much wrong she could do there, but trimming the dead from the living parts of the flowers was a different matter altogether. Some of them were easy cuts, like the brown, twig-looking thing that streaked across the blue, or the piece that looked like a hungry caterpillar had spent all day munching on it. But she was afraid of cutting too much off and ended up passing on more pieces than she actually cut.

When she stood up half an hour later, she was satisfied she had not killed any of the flowers. They would last until Elizabeth's next weekly visit.

She picked up the bag of clippings to compost in the backyard and beamed down at her garden one last time before heading inside. They were all still alive. She'd never been able to make it to the start of summer with all her flowers before. That had to be a good omen. It was going to be a good summer.

Elizabeth knocked on the door as Ryan ran down the stairs. Ryan had changed into a Captain America tank top and had switched out her earrings for a darker pair that matched the leather bracelet she hurried to strap onto her wrist.

"Slow down," May called. "You have plenty of time!"

Ryan didn't listen, but slammed one hand against the doorframe as she ripped it open with the other.

"Oh!" Elizabeth exclaimed, startled. "Ryan. Those are lovely. Where did you get them?"

"Mom got them for me," she said, craning her neck to see the street behind the adult in her way. "Did you see Stacy?"

"She's circling around now," Elizabeth answered, stepping inside.

"Cool. Thanks, Mrs. Stracke!" Ryan started out the door.

"Text me before and after!" May shouted as the door closed.

Elizabeth shook her head. "Teenagers. Can't get a word in with them."

The door flung back open. "I will, Mom. And uhh . . . keys?"

"Table by the couch."

Ryan ran into the living room, then reappeared a second later and raced outside as May said, "I'll lock it."

The door closed with a hurried "thanks!"

"Need any help making dinner?" Elizabeth asked.

May shook her head. "I need to cut up some of Chris's bread, but aside from that we're ready."

"Chris made bread?" Elizabeth's eyes widened. Like everyone else around, she loved Chris's bread.

"Made it this morning," May said, entering the kitchen. "Asked me to bring it with me when I picked them up today, but then he texted around lunchtime saying not to bother."

"Oh. It was for *her*, wasn't it?"

Scott must have told her about Lisa breaking up with Chris.

"Yeah," Chris said from the doorway.

Elizabeth turned. "I'm sorry, Chris. Scott told me . . ." She trailed off, either unable or unwilling to say what happened. Instead, she opened her arms and pulled him into a hug.

"It's alright," he said, putting on a brave face in front of Elizabeth. He made her so proud. Smiling like that even after his girlfriend left him for another man. And on the last day of school—in the cafeteria of all places! "It's better I found out now than later."

"Right you are," May said.

"You deserve better."

Elizabeth released Chris and stepped back. "They grow up so fast, don't they? I remember when you and Scott first started playing together. The two of you were hardly three feet tall then, tottering all over the place, but now look at you. Baking like a pro and working through terrible people with grace."

"Thanks." Chris looked around Elizabeth to May. "Have you seen my keys?"

"Honestly, what is it with you two and keys?" May asked. "They're with the mail."

"Thanks, Mom."

"Have fun," Elizabeth said.

"Meet new people," May said. "Text before and after."

"You too!"

The door closed.

"Do you know where they decided to eat?" May asked. Last she'd heard, they were either going to Jackie's Pizza or Mexican Food, a food truck that sold great, big, greasy tacos. Both were in the same strip as the bar/coffee house the band would be playing at later in the evening.

"I think Anthony wanted to try out Mexican Food."

"Anthony?" May was sure she'd heard that name before, but had she ever met the boy? She didn't think so. Had to be one of Maxine's friends.

"Scott met him last year. He works at Guitar Center. They apparently hit it off while Scott was waiting for a lesson. Oh, and he'll be the one replacing Maxine in the band."

"Huh." May remembered where she had heard the name then. Scott had talked about him before. He thought Chris and Anthony would get along well, but they hadn't been able to make a night out together work.

"Have you met him before?" May asked.

"Once. A few months ago. His school's bus broke down—Jasper," she said, explaining it all. Jasper was the drug den of a high school May escaped from, and it had not improved at all since she left it. The state's solution? Slash the budget and hope the dealers leave. It hadn't happened yet, and Jasper remained one of the poorest schools there was. "So, Scott called and asked if he could skip calculus review to take him home. I said no, of course, but offered to get the boy. He's nice. Funny too. Chris will like him, I'm sure of that."

It looked like Chris would be meeting new people after all tonight. May smiled. It was good she'd forced him out.

May cut the bread while she told Elizabeth about her latest piece for the paper. It wasn't much, just the usual fluff piece her editor loved for the Life Section. Readers wrote in each week and she gave them advice. It was usually the same: be open, honest, and a good person, and it will work out. And if something is preventing you from being that open, honest, and good person, get it out of your life. But every so often she got interesting ones. She had one last week from a recently single mother asking what to do with her children for their first summer since their dad had passed.

She liked those the best—not the ones with dead parents, but the ones that made her stop and think, that made her question if she was actually qualified to be writing to these people. Whenever she got letters like that, she had to open herself up to them. Be completely open, honest, and good. Letters like that made her actually follow her own advice.

There was nothing like that this week. The one she just sent in was from a middle-aged woman who caught her husband cheating and was asking what she could do to make it right.

"Matt would be out the door before he could pull his pants on if he ever did that," Elizabeth said. "I know he won't," she added, interrupting May. "But that doesn't change the fact that she should've kicked him between the legs, then tossed him out."

"As much as I agree with you, I can't be that blatant." They moved to the table. "If I just say he's a cheat, give him the boot, there's three ways she and others will react. The first is, 'Yeah he is,' but the other two will be sympathetic to him. One will say there's more to the story, and the other will say she should forgive him, and I don't want that woman leaving the column with anything but the right answer. And none of that is to mention I'm an advice column writer, not an answer . . . giver?" May wasn't quite sure where she meant to go with that last part.

"Answerer," Elizabeth corrected, covering her mouth and laughing through a mouthful of Chris's bread. "But I get what you're saying. You need them to get to the right answer without explicitly telling them."

From there the conversation shifted to being about Matt and his trip, then to plans for the summer, and how on earth they were going to get the boys to get their college applications ready on time. They decided on bribery and a lot of reminding and prodding.

Elizabeth insisted on helping May clean up and by the time they were done, it was almost nine o'clock. May's phone buzzed:

bout 2 start.

"They're about to go on," May said, then sent back a quick *Thanks!* She could ask about Anthony, but no. She would do that in the morning.

Elizabeth and May sent Scott and Maxine a quick *Good Luck!!!*

It was a ritual they had for whenever they could not make it to a concert. Usually, if they did not go it was because it was too late. Elizabeth liked to joke it was because she was too old to blend in with the crowd. She'd then turn to May and ask what her excuse was—she could still fit in after all. And May would then admit she had no excuse. It was just past her bedtime already.

"I would go, but I've always been told to avoid being the oldest, or youngest person at a party," Elizabeth said, continuing their tradition.

"Come on, you're not that old. I'm sure there'll be some grandparents sleeping in the corner. You'll fit right in."

"And what's your excuse?"

"Me? None. I'm right with the grandparents. In fact—" May's phone buzzed again. It was Chris: *British Hamlets starting 9 HBO btw.*

"Who is it?" Elizabeth asked.

"Tennant's Hamlet is playing tonight," May said. "Chris just texted."

Elizabeth's eyes got wide. She loved Shakespeare about as much as May, plus the movie version with David Tennant was one of the best around. Everyone agreed to that.

"Want to watch it?"

"I will never turn down Shakespeare," Elizabeth smiled. "I might fall asleep, but let's watch it."

Thank you! May texted Chris.

"Any idea how he found out about it? Elizabeth asked.

"I am not sure. Let me text him."

Who told you about it?

His response came as the opening credits began:

Anthony
Scott's friend

May laughed and showed the phone to Elizabeth. She was liking this Anthony guy already. And by the look of it, Chris was too.

Chris woke them up when he opened the front door. "Hey, Mom."

May yawned. They must have both fallen asleep during the movie. The last thing she remembered was Hamlet killing Polonius.

"Hey." She rolled to a sitting position on the couch. She powered through another yawn and asked, "How was the concert."

"Fine."

Chris turned to the stairs.

"What about Anthony? That's his name, right? How do—"

"—I'm kind of tired, Mom," he interrupted her. "Can we talk about it in the morning? I just want to get some sleep."

"Oh . . . Yes. Get some rest."

"Good night."

"Good night."

Elizabeth stirred in time to mumble "good night" after his retreating footsteps.

"Good night," he called back down.

Elizabeth chuckled as she stretched and stood. "Like I said: can't ever get a word in with them."

May just nodded in answer.

She walked Elizabeth to the door and closed it behind her.

May checked her phone, heading back into the living room. There were two texts from Ryan and one from Chris.

Chris and Ryan each sent one saying the concert was over and they were on their way back home. Those were an hour apart, Chris had probably stayed behind with Scott and his friend, and Ryan had sent another about forty-five minutes ago: it was of May asleep on the couch. Little clip-art *Zs* drifted from her head and the caption *Good Night! Sleep Tight!* was at the top.

She was home then. That was good. May could go back to sleep.

She turned off the TV and lights, then headed upstairs.

Ryan's lights were still on, so May knocked on the door to say good night.

Ryan was lying on the bed, propped up on her elbows with her phone in hand. She looked up and smiled.

"Hang on. Mom's here." She was facetiming Maxine and turned the phone so Maxine could see her too.

"Hey, Ms. Flowers!"

"Hello, Maxine. I heard you guys did great."

Maxine blushed for a moment, before the screen blurred then went to black. "Don't even. I was sharp on *Fishies*."

"No one could notice but you," Ryan assured her, turning the screen back to her.

"Whatever. You're just saying that because you owe me."

"No!" But she smiled: whatever it was she owed Maxine for, Ryan was definitely in debt for something.

May shook her head and held back a smile. *Kids.*

"I just wanted to say good night."

"Good night," the two girls said.

May closed the door and found herself collapsing into her own bed within minutes.

The next morning, Chris was quiet. He asked if he could cook lunch and dinner. That was not good. Him cooking one meal was just because he enjoyed it, but he only ever requested to cook every meal when there was something on his mind. Chris liked to cook as a means of relieving stress. As much as May hoped the concert would push Lisa from his head, he had to still be thinking about her. It had only been a day, she knew that, but that didn't change the fact that she wanted Chris to be happy without that *cheating*—without the cloud of Lisa hanging over him.

May tried to find out more about Anthony, but Chris did not seem eager to talk. She tried asking about the concert, but only got short answers in response. Chris only opened up once Ryan came downstairs. She talked about the movie, the good guys won in the end, then about the concert—they closed with Maxine's favorite song—"I Wanted to Write a Love Song"—and she was even able to tell May a little bit about Anthony. When she brought up the other boy, Chris had to leave. He needed to check on the curry cooking in the kitchen.

While he was gone, Ryan told her Anthony and Chris seemed like they were getting along well. She saw them sitting together at the coffee bar whenever she looked over, and when it was time to go backstage to congratulate the band on another good concert, she was pretty sure she saw them exchange numbers before heading back.

They ate lunch and Chris didn't talk much, but something changed with him in the afternoon. He and Ryan had cleaned the kitchen while May went upstairs to start a load of laundry. When she came down, her children were hugging. That made her day—her week. Ryan was able to shake Chris from his funk. He smiled when they parted.

May did not ask what they were talking about, not then, but she made a note to make Ryan some cookies for being there for Chris. She wouldn't say that's what they were for, Chris could eat them too if he wanted any, but she'd make them black forest, Ryan's favorite.

When it was time to make dinner, Chris asked for her help. That almost made her as happy as seeing Ryan and Chris holding each other. He never cooked with her when he was upset. Never. Cooking together was always for happy times. They only did it when things were good. And that meant whatever Ryan said got through to Chris.

He was done feeling sorry for himself. Maybe she should have been a little worried that he got over Lisa so fast, but she wasn't going to complain about it.

Chris was quiet when they began cooking. He didn't say a single thing as they loaded up the kitchen island with all the materials needed.

He stepped back from the island and surveyed the array of ingredients; face blank. He normally had a big smile right about now; he would be thinking about what they were about to make and how good it would taste, but right now . . . maybe he wasn't quite over Lisa.

"Can you cut the chicken breasts while I make the bread crumbs?" he asked.

"Sure thing, sweetie."

"They just need to be halves," he said, but that was all he said. No joke or explanation of why turning the breasts into halves was an important step in his cooking magic. He also didn't say what he was doing while she worked. He grabbed the spices, almost mindlessly, and sprinkled pinches and bunches into the small mixing bowl.

She had to focus on her own task though. She cut the breasts perfectly in half, making sure to keep herself to as high of a standard as he would have on a better day. On any other day.

When she was close to finishing, Chris pulled out a few ingredients and set them in front of her.

"Then mix these all together until they're smooth. For the sauce."

She slid the stack of breast-halves to him and started on the sauce. She was all but finished when he finally spoke.

"Hey, Mom?"

He slid the chicken breast back and forth across his hands even though it was already covered in the bread crumbs and spices. May stopped mixing the sauce and looked at him. Odd. He didn't meet her eye but stared down at the counter.

"What would you think if . . . hypothetically, if I . . ."

He set the breast down and looked down toward the table as if checking back over all the ingredients they'd brought out.

"What is it, sweetie?"

He sighed.

"What if . . ." He looked up to her. "I got a job."

She tracked his eyes back to the table. Was he ashamed of asking that? Why would he be worried about asking her permission to earn some money? Unless . . . it would mean quitting work at St. Peters.

"What about Peter's?" May asked. The kids loved him there. Sure, the job didn't pay, but they weren't that strapped for cash and she did give him a decent allowance for helping around the house. Plus, he could always help out the neighbors for money like he'd done last summer.

"I could do both," he said, his shoulders slumping.

"I'm not against it." She tried to reassure Chris, make him stand up straight, be happy like he was with Ryan earlier. "What did you have in mind?"

"I don't know." His head went down even further. "Waiting tables or something."

"And those jobs usually work nights."

It could work. His job at Peter's was in the mid-morning to a little bit after lunch. He could do both if he wanted. "Have you seen anyplace hiring?"

Unfortunately, he'd probably waited a little too long to find a summer job. Most of the positions she knew about would have already been filled.

Chris shook his head.

"Do you think Mrs. Asim's hiring?" May asked.

Chris shrugged. "I can ask Scott."

Ryan came into the kitchen. "Smells good. Oh, and Mom? I have everything but that sheet folded."

"Honestly, Ryan." May shook her head. "You're going to have to learn to fold a fitted sheet one of these days."

"Only moms know how to do those," she shrugged. "It's one of your powers or something."

"I'll be back," May said. "Ryan, do whatever Chef Chris needs while I'm gone."

As May left, she heard Ryan whisper.

"You talk to her yet?"

What was that about? Chris must have talked with Ryan about getting a job.

That made her smile again. They would always have each other. No matter what happened, Ryan would always be there to support her brother. Whether that was dealing with cheaters, or giving him the courage to ask about quitting volunteer work in favor of a paying job, Ryan would help Chris out whenever he didn't think he could talk with her.

Chapter 2

The Heart is a Cannibal

CHRIS SLEPT IN. THAT was unusual for him, especially on a Sunday. But, he was dressed and ready when it was time to leave for Mass. It was Father Lee's last service with them and the pews were packed, though May had her suspicions that many of the people were just showing up for the free lunch after Mass.

Father Lee gave a nice homily. It was about finding the good in all things. May kept waiting for him to tie in his departure, but he never did. Instead, he talked about looking for God in upcoming struggles and finding the light in all dark places.

At the end of the service, he introduced his replacement: Father Green, a young black man who looked to be fresh out of seminary. His hair was short on the sides and long on the top, and during the dismissal, when Father Green walked past, May caught a glimpse of black boots beneath his robe.

Boots? May didn't know how she felt about that. The new father was clearly not traditional, probably more liberal than Father Lee was, but he could also be good for the youth of the church. As great as Father Lee was, May had noticed he didn't do so well with the younger members of the church. Most people left the Confirmation courses with at least one story about how the awkward Father Lee accidentally did something a bit creepy.

Those stories usually involved the poor father trying to make a pop culture reference only to find out it did not mean what he thought it meant.

May wanted to meet the new father, so they proceeded to the lunch. Chris and Ryan left to find Maxine and Scott, while May worked her way toward the two men in black.

"Ah, there she is," Father Lee greeted her. "Just the woman I wanted to see. I was just telling Jackson here about the movers and shakers of this place."

Jackson Green. So that was his full name. He extended his hand and May shook it.

"Father Lee tells me you're the one I should talk to about bake sales."

"My son does most of the baking, but I do the planning. He's around here somewhere," May added, anticipating his next question.

Father Green nodded. "Is he a chef?"

"We really need to figure that one out. He has until the end of the summer to decide, but he doesn't know yet. He loves to cook, but isn't sure if he wants to be a full-time chef."

"What does he want to do instead?"

"No clue. Something with science, but . . ." Something with science was incredibly vague.

"Father Lee?" Suzanne, one of the other older congregants, called, nudging her way through the crowd to them. She was short and tried to make up for her height with a beehive hairdo and those large hats that were fluffed up by colored feathers, but it just made her stature more obvious. Only good thing about them was how they distracted from her overpowering perfume. The old woman smelled as though a florist had decided to also break into taxidermy.

"Father Lee," she said, leaning in close. "We are running low on punch."

Father Lee met her grave stare with an easy smile. After nearly two decades working at St. Peter's, he was used to her intensity.

"I believe there is more in the back. I can help bring it out." He added quickly when Suzanne looked as though he'd just struck her. "I'll be right back," he promised.

Once they were out of earshot, Father Green said, "I have to be honest with you May; we weren't just talking about bake sales before. Lee was just about to tell me how he helped save you, or some such."

The blood started rushing to May's head. She glanced at the ground, her gaze fixing on his shiny black boots. Why couldn't she look at him though? It's not like the father had lied, or as if no one knew about her and Cesar.

"I didn't . . ." Father Green started. "I'm sorry if I brought up any bad memories. I think everyone deserves a fresh start; no matter what's happened. That's the whole point of confession, after all."

"It's alright. I don't even know why I'm embarrassed—everyone knows. I've practically talked about it to everyone here before."

The father nodded. His eyes flicked over behind her shoulder. Suzanne was gesturing wildly to move everyone out of her way. "How about her? Is she always like that?"

"Ever since I've been here."

"How long has that been?"

"About eighteen years now. I started attending shortly after Chris was born."

"Oh, does your husband attend as well?"

"No." May shook her head. "He died the day Chris was born."

"Oh." Father Green had that same look everyone did when they heard about that. He didn't know what to say, he had nothing to say except for the same "I'm sorry for your loss" everyone gave.

"It's alright. He died in a car accident," May said, once again anticipating the question that always came next.

"And Father Lee visited you in the hospital?" he guessed, probably in part to change the subject.

"No, but that's a story for—"

"Mom?" Ryan came up from behind her. Father Green looked between them—their stark difference in appearance threw most people, but he regained his composure quickly enough. Almost everyone had that reaction the first time they saw the two of them together.

"Father Green, this is my daughter, Ryan."

"Nice to meet you, sir." Ryan reached out her hand, brushing away all the tension of Father Green's confusion.

"I guess now's as good a time as any," May said. "Ryan's parents took me in when I was pregnant. They pretty much adopted me as their own daughter, got me off drugs, and led me to the church. They've been looking out for me ever since."

"But, they died when I was six," Ryan said, picking up the story. "They're still my parents, but Mom's my mom too—it's always been that way."

May couldn't do anything but smile at that. She loved Ryan, and Ryan loved her back. That was all that mattered to them.

"Henry and Stephanie left me everything they had." Enough to pay for both the kids' college and then some. "And, I've used that to ensure our children have a better life than I did."

"That's amazing," Father Green said.

"And here's the little man that started it all." Chris was walking toward them. "Chris, this is Father Green."

"Pleasure to meet you, Chris." They shook hands.

"You too, umm . . ." Chris said, turning from the priest. "They left. Mrs. Stracke had errands to run."

May nodded. There went that lunch plan. "Father, would you like to have lunch with us?"

Father Green looked around the cafeteria briefly before catching sight of Father Lee surrounded by Suzanne's gaggle of women. "Sure. I'd love to."

Their progress to the buffet line was slowed by the countless hands and greetings offered to the new father; however, most people let Father Green pass without much trouble. The crowd did give her enough time to mix an Arnold Palmer without holding up the line too much. After getting her favorite drink, they moved to sit around a small, square table. Father Green took the chair with its back to a majority of the crowd, and May sat across from him with her children on either side.

After a moment of looking down at their food, Father Green asked, "Ryan? Would you like to lead us in prayer?"

May glanced up from the food. That's odd. Most of the time, the father would say grace for everyone.

"Oh, uhh . . ." Ryan shared May's puzzlement. She looked from the father to her mother. "Sure?"

They made the sign of the cross, Ryan hesitated then began, "Bless us o' Lord for these our gifts," Father Green joined in, and they said the rest of the prayer together.

"Amen."

Ryan glanced at Father Green after they made the sign of the cross again.

"First time praying for a priest?"

"Yeah."

"Did it feel any different?"

"I mean, it felt awkward, but I guess not."

"Why didn't you pray?" Chris asked.

Father Green lowered his head, his cheeks looked like they were flushing red. He really was young.

"There'll be a whole sermon on that," he promised. "That belief of mine comes from Matthew 23 with some pneumatology mixed in, but that's a conversation for another time. For now, suffice to say I believe everyone should lead prayer in their life. And, if you can pray for your priest, then surely you can pray for your neighbor."

"I like that," May said. It was a nice thought, even though she was not too comfortable praying over a priest yet. But that was the point, so maybe she would in time.

The kids began eating.

Father Green nodded. "I've noticed most members of the laity love the idea, but a lot of the clergy I've met think it's too liberal."

"You have any other liberal beliefs?" Ryan asked between forkfuls of mashed potato.

"Like what?"

"Oh, I don't know. How about the big ones, like same-sex marriage?"

Chris shot her a look and May did the same. They both knew that type of talk had no place at lunch, especially in front of a priest.

"I think," Father Green spoke slowly, carefully thinking through each word. "I think that is a complicated question. One in which the Gospels do not directly lend their voice to. Instead, we have to look at tradition, culture, and a whole lot of other things." He stopped talking, but his short answer ended more in trailing off than on a definitive note. "If you would like to talk more about it, I would be glad to meet with you in private," he added, somewhat meekly.

"What about you, Mom?" Ryan asked. What was she doing? Did she not know where they were? "What do you think?"

"Sex is for procreation," she said. They had to leave this subject as quickly as possible. "That's all."

"I need to go to the restroom," Chris mumbled quickly, standing.

Father Green looked worryingly at Chris as he left, "Is he . . . ?"

"That's what he told Lisa," Ryan said, shooting May a glare. "May I go?"

"Make sure he's okay. And tell him he did the right thing, telling Lisa that."

Father Green raised an eyebrow at May.

"I'm sorry, Father. My son's—his girlfriend cheated on him because he wanted to wait."

"Ah," Father Green said. When May did not say anything in return, he added, "You have a good son. If there's anything I can do for him, please don't hesitate to let me know."

"Thank you, Father. I like to think he would have made his father proud."

"What was he like?"

"Foolish—like a kid in that way. He always tried to make everyone happy, but ended up getting himself in trouble along the way. He could always talk his way out of it though. People just couldn't stay mad at him like that. One time the principal caught Cesar high off his head, with a fresh bowl of pot in his office. He got off with a warning. No detention or anything."

"Really?"

"Of course that's a testament to Jasper High as much as it is to his character."

"Jasper High, that's the local school, right?"

"Yes, but most of the kids here go to St. Francis—that's the parochial school."

"I'll be leading Mass there in the fall. Is it a good school?"

"Wonderful. They treat the staff well, have good parental involvement, and have good scores."

Plus, they gave both her children full rides so they could attend.

"How are the sports?"

"Football and basketball are okay. Soccer's the only great team though, and the rest are nothing to see."

"I studied sports ministry before seminary," he explained. "I want to try and start a team or something here, and I want to try and reach out to the coaches at the school."

"Oh, I'm sure they'd love that. I know the band would, the director keeps complaining that they aren't Christian enough from what the kids tell me, but I'm not sure if you'd be interested in that."

"It could be a good start," Father Green finished eating and pushed the plate in front of himself so he could lean forward and rest his elbows on the table. "What instruments do they play?"

May laughed. "Goodness, Father, you just like to know everything don't you?"

"Getting to know people is my favorite part of the job." He shrugged.

May smiled at the new father. He would do well at St. Peter's. Father Lee had been good, but he never took the time to learn much about those who didn't work for him. If this lunch was any indication, Father Green would be different.

"Chris plays guitar a bit and helps out with the drumline parts for marching season, and Ryan played trumpet last year, but won't be doing it next year." The fine arts requirement was two semesters, and Ryan said from August all the way through registration that two semesters would be more than enough for her.

May's phone buzzed.

"That might be the kids," May said. "Mind if I . . .?"

"Go on ahead."

May took out the phone. There was a message from Ryan: *Took Chris on walk round church*

She sent back: *Okay. Tell Chris I love him.*

"Everything okay?" Father Green asked.

May nodded, "But if I start talking about it, I'll have to talk about her, and if that happens we'll have to go to confession afterward."

"Ah, well, let's talk about something else then."

"How about you, Father. What's your story?"

"Not much to tell in all honesty. I have three older siblings. The oldest is my sister, Alicia. She's about ten years older than me. She's married and has one son, and they live about an hour away from here, up in—"

"I thought we were talking about you?" May said. "Sorry," she added quickly, realizing that she'd just interrupted a priest.

"It's alright," he waved a hand, "but as I said. There's not much to tell. I never did anything fun as a kid, being raised by my parents and two sisters kept me out of trouble. I went to UConn for my undergrad, then moved out to Colorado for seminary. After getting ordained, I was a priest in Denver for a few years before getting assigned here. As I said, not much interesting there."

May tried to do the math in her head. How old did that make him? Four years before seminary, then some time at another church . . . he could be thirty-something. Maybe mid-twenties.

"I'm thirty," Father Green said, as if he got that question every time he told his life story.

"Oh." Thirty? Not too much younger than herself then.

"Father Green!" Suzanne bustled toward them. Her feathered hat fanned the decay of skunk and rose to them as she half-ran. "Father Green! Some of the ladies and I were wondering if you could take a picture with us and the father."

Father Green glanced from the dyed, auburn beehive above her head to May who gave a quick nod of encouragement. She did not know why Suzanne absolutely needed to have Father Green take the photo for her, she probably wanted to talk to him about some terrible slight one of the other parishioners did to her on their way over, but it was best to not get on her bad side.

"I should be heading out as it is." May stood. "It was a pleasure to meet you, father."

"The pleasure was all mine." Father Green stood and they shook hands. "And please tell Chris he can always talk to me if he'd like, no matter what it is."

"Chris wanted to say something," Ryan said.

"Oh, alright." May pulled the key out of the ignition. They were stopped in the driveway. Chris looked out the window, away from her.

"I'll be in my room," Ryan said. She stepped out of the car and headed toward the house. Strange. What could Chris be asking? Had he changed his mind about the job? Or maybe he had found one and wanted her permission before taking it. Only one way to find out . . .

"What did you want to talk about?" May asked.

He turned to her, but didn't look up. His gaze seemed stuck on her Rosary bracelet: a Mother's Day gift from a few years ago. When he'd given it to her, Chris said she was the best mom he could have. He could always count on her. She'd laughed. It was the most cliché thing he'd ever said to her. The best thing, too.

Now something was wrong. Something had happened to her boy. He had to know she would be there for him.

"Chris?"

His reply was soft, faint and distant. His head ducked so low that his chin touched his chest.

"I'm gay."

"What?" her response sounded just as distant. Like it came from outside the car.

"I'm gay."

May had spent years wishing she had a car. She had sat in front of the AC, turned it on full blast, and closed her eyes to pretend like the cold air was wind rushing past on the highway. Her parents had yelled at her whenever they caught her doing it, but it was always worth it. The air had felt so good shooting up her arms, small little goose bumps rising up from wrist to shoulder, taking each hair with it in the chill.

That was the next best thing to getting high at the time. The AC had never failed to send little shivers across her body. She'd come to associate that feeling with being free. In front of the AC, it was like she could be heading anywhere. She was ready to grab Cesar and get out of town.

Sitting in the car with Chris, the dead, still air of the car clamped around her. Goosebumps spread across her clammy arms, but nothing followed it.

"Sweetie, what are you talking about?

Chris raised his head just enough for her to see the rims of his eyes. Not enough to see his face, to see him smile or frown at what must be a failed joke. What, please God, had to be a failed joke. But he hid his smile from her, lowered his head, and kept even the rims of his eyes hidden from her.

"I think I'm gay."

"No you're not." She forced a short laugh. Why was he insisting on this? Chris wasn't gay. Couldn't be. He was a good kid; knew right from wrong. He'd just gone to Mass! He was Christian, same as her and Ryan.

"Mom."

"You aren't gay, Chris. You dated Lisa—this isn't because of her, is it?"

"No!" He shouted, crossing his arms. They loomed like a wall between them. His voice was louder, but it wasn't any clearer. It shook with the weight of his breathing.

"Why would you do this?"

What could he gain from lying to her like this? He should've known she wouldn't approve of him making things up. Aside from cursing, lying was one of the few things that got money put into the curse jar.

"I didn't want this."

She shook her head, looking out to the garden. Could Chris actually think he was gay? He wouldn't lie to her, not about this. But if he wasn't doing this on purpose, why even talk with her about it?

"What's the problem then?" There had to be something else wrong. Chris had to know homosexuality was wrong. There was no reason for him to choose that path.

"Mom, it's not a problem. It's. That's . . ." He shifted against the door, as far away as physically possible without leaving the car. "You aren't listening." The answer came out as a low mumble.

For whatever reason, the sound of his voice caught her breath.

Oh, Chris . . .

This was hard for him too. She should have seen that. She should have kept her calm, reacted better. He was confused, maybe even scared about what this would mean for them. He had to know what he was thinking was wrong and he had come to her for help—not chastisement.

"I'm sorry, Chris." She reached over to him. His hand was cold in her own. "This doesn't mean I don't love you."

Only then did he look up, his eyes red and puffy around their edges. How could he have been scared of her abandoning him? Whatever mistake he had made, it could be undone. He was not lost. They could get help. Get him back to normal.

"I could never stop loving you, sweetie. No matter what mistakes you make—"

"—mistakes?"

"They don't define you. You can get over this, Chris. I know you can. We'll get you whatever help you need. Okay?"

He didn't nod. But why was he just staring through her? They would work through this together.

"I can call the father and get us set up with an appointment."

He didn't nod to that either. What was he thinking? Why wouldn't he talk to her, let her help him?

"Chris?"

"Can I go inside?"

Why did those words hit her the hardest? He held his head level, his eyes now fixed above her head to the felt covered ceiling. He was not crying, but he was about to; jaw taut, almost shaking.

She nodded. "Yes."

That was all she could say. She tried to say more, but her throat seized and cracked her voice. A swelling lump cut off the rest of her words and if she forced it aside and said what she needed to say anyway, then the tears would start right then and there in front of Chris. She shouldn't do that. As much as she wanted to assure him that it would be okay, she could not cry. He needed her to be strong, to show him everything would be fine and that no matter what, no matter what he thought or feared, they would get through this together.

He slouched out of the car.

"Chris, I love you . . ."

Her voice cracked. It would have been worth it if he had smiled. She could have justified her already running eyes if he had smiled, said the words back to her, or done anything but turn to her, face twisted up, crumpled in on itself, and shed the tears she'd feared would come from herself.

Chapter 3

How to Explain

MAY STAYED IN THE car after Chris left. She wanted to run after him, wrap him up in a hug and tell him . . . tell him *something*. Anything that would show him, show them both, that everything would be okay. But she couldn't. She did not know what to say, how to say it, or how to do anything but sit in her car. Right now that was the only option she had. Every other path led right back to Chris's red eyes and her without anything to say.

She had to figure it out first. What to say and how to say it. Anything to stop what had just happened from happening again. She could do that.

"God, let me be able to do that." She had been praying ever since Chris closed the door. She'd started with her decade bracelet, moving the beads slowly between her fingers as she slipped from one prayer to the next until she finished all five loops of the Rosary. Afterwards, she was no closer to finding any answers or guidance. She'd switched to free-style prayers.

Father Lee had always said it was good she could do those. Most Catholics, he'd said, couldn't pray without following a script. May though—she'd never had that problem. Praying was always spontaneous, one-sided, and mostly asking for things but never following a set path. She'd prayed that way ever since coming to St. Peter's. Her personal prayer style had never failed her in Chris's eighteen years.

But in all that time she had never actually prayed for guidance. Now, the one time she needed God to answer, God kept silent. Then again, had God ever responded to her? Really responded?

Father Lee had always said the trick to praying was more in the listening than anything else. He had always compared it to meditating; directing your mind and heart to God and putting yourself in the right place. Getting to that right place could be done in a few ways. You could pray, meditate, or talk with a member of the clergy.

May opened her eyes. That was it. She needed to talk with Father Lee. A simple phone call would do it. He might not be back from the lunch yet, but she could always leave a message. She could just say she needed to speak with him and not have to give any details over the phone.

She called, but the voice on the answering machine was not Father Lee's. It was younger, happier unlike the stiff greeting all St. Peter's was accustomed to. The new priest, Father Green, had already replaced the message with his own.

May hung up without a message. It was too soon to request a meeting over the phone. Who knows how he would react to the news of Chris's struggle? No, this was better kept in the family for now. If Chris needed more guidance they could talk on Sunday. But for now, they would work it out themselves. No need for everyone else to hear about this.

May left the car and headed inside. Ryan stood by the entryway stairs.

"What happened?" she asked before May could clear the threshold. "All he'll say is that he told you."

"You knew?"

As soon as the words left her mouth, she realized her guess was right. Ryan had left them in the car and forced the conversation between them. That must have been what they were talking about yesterday as well. That was good then. Ryan was helping to keep Chris out of trouble.

"He told me at the concert."

"Does anyone else know?"

"No." She shook her head. "I don't think so. No one else except Lisa, that is. Chris won't tell me everything about that, but he told her he was having thoughts or something and I think that's why she cheated on him."

That stopped her where she stood, her hand on the lock. So this was Lisa's fault; one question out of the way. Chris must have wanted to wait, but Lisa had convinced him that desire for chastity made him gay. Then, to top it all off, she had cheated on him. Someone really ought to have a word with the girl's parents. They should have raised her better. At least it wasn't too late for Chris: he had told her and they could get help.

"But Mom, what happened?"

May didn't answer. She had to be careful with how she phrased what needed to be said. She had to let Ryan know she still loved Chris, that this mistake changed nothing. Besides, they would be getting him help. Still, she had to let Ryan know she would never let sinful behavior stand in their house. She would do everything she could to keep them safe.

"He told me what he's been struggling with."

"And?"

"I said we would talk to the father about it."

More questions would need to be answered, but for now that would be enough.

"Okay, but like, how did you say that? I mean, did you say it like *I love you no matter what and accept you and this is just a thing* way? Or, like in a *you're grounded until school* kind of way?"

"This isn't a joke, Ryan."

"No it's not, but neither of you seem to be telling me what really happened."

"We talked—"

"—and he came in crying."

"I don't like your tone."

"And I don't like you hiding things from me." Ryan folded her arms across her chest. Her usual smile was gone without a trace. Instead, she wore a deep scowl.

May took a breath before trusting herself to speak. "You're right." For them to get through this, they had to be completely honest with each other. "I told him this doesn't define him and I'll love him no matter how long it takes to get back to normal."

"Wait, so you think it's wrong?"

"It is wrong."

"But—"

"—Ryan, I cannot have this conversation with you now. It's a sin, plain as that, but that does not mean we can't help Chris. That's what I intend to do and I expect you to do the same."

Ryan glared at her for a moment, then turned and grumbled something as she headed into the living room.

May would have to talk with her about her attitude later. For now, though, she had to go and check on Chris. She would not yell at Ryan. Even though her grumbling was unacceptable, it was understandable. It was already a long day and it was only noon.

She stopped outside Chris's door. No sound escaped through the gap between carpet and wood. May knocked and waited, her hand wrapped around the doorknob.

"Chris?" she pushed the door in slowly.

He lay on his bed beneath his red, quilted comforter. The cover's slight breath of movement was the only sign he was there; even his head was covered by the blankets. Could he get air? She leaned in. A gap faced the wall where his head should be.

"Chris." She sat down on the bed and rested a hand on the quaking covers. She could not hear him crying, but what else could he be doing? His eyes would be red, nose runny and sticky. Weird how that image could hurt so much more than anything he could say. She would give anything to get his head back out of the covers.

For everything to go back to the way it was.

The next day, Chris announced he wanted to speak with Father Green after church, and May agreed. Surely, the father would be able to fix this. He could talk with Chris in the ways she did not know how, to show him homosexuality was a sin, or to help explain his gay thoughts.

Despite her certainty that everything would be solved in a week, May found it impossible to concentrate on her work. Chris was drifting away from her. He hardly spoke at all anymore. And not just with her; he spent most of his time in his room. Even when she forced him outside, he only tramped out to the backyard and stared at the grass.

But everything would be fixed by Monday. At the very least, Chris would start up his summer volunteer work at St. Peter's on Monday. He would start talking then, if not before. May was sure of it.

But for that week, there was nothing she could do. Ryan could hardly talk with him herself. She certainly could not open him up during lunch or dinner. The three of them ended up spending their meals mostly in silence. Ryan tried to talk, but their few conversations never lasted more than a few exchanges.

The only thing that kept May together was gardening with Elizabeth. While they sat in the dirt, May found herself saying, "I'm having trouble with Chris." Why say what kind of trouble exactly? No need to spread word of Chris's struggle yet. Especially not since the father would be helping out on Sunday.

Elizabeth laughed and assured her there was nothing to worry about. Teenagers were aloof by nature. Scott had gone through the same phase himself last summer, if she'd remember. And May did remember that. Scott had spent a good month sulking. He'd hardly spoken with Chris during that time.

Maybe what was happening with Chris was perfectly normal. He was just having a troubling time. In a week, it would be behind him. He would come back to himself and could go on living like he had before Lisa stormed into his life.

That Sunday, the tension between them was still there. A knot had been forming in her chest all week and it felt like it was about to burst.

The only thing Chris said during the ride to Mass was, "Can I talk with Father Green afterward?"

May nodded. As if just being reminded about their arrangement. Like she hadn't been thinking about it all week.

She could hardly think about anything else during the service. Father Green's homily passed by her. Words of hope and redemption. Funny anecdotes that got the congregation to laugh together. The whole while she kept her hands folded neatly together in her lap and prayed.

God, please let their conversation go well. Help put this all behind him.

While everyone else was filing out of the chapel, May, Chris, and Ryan stayed seated. Once the crowd had dwindled to the last stragglers, May turned to Chris.

"We'll be right outside," she promised.

Ryan squeezed his hand, but did not say anything. She stood and left Chris in the emptying sanctuary. Father Green saw them leaving Chris behind. He raised his eyebrows, as if questioning whether or not she had forgotten her son. She met his gaze and he understood, or at least he lowered his brows and shook one last hand before calling: "Chris, would you mind helping me with the hymnals?"

May smiled. The father was using one of the oldest tricks in the book. When she was pregnant with Chris, a younger Father Lee had asked her to help with the pews. That same excuse led to her salvation, her conversion. It was the first step to learning the correct path lay in Christian teachings.

The church lobby was crowded. Families huddled in packs with smaller children tugging lightly at their parents' sleeves; the older kids crowded in groups off to the side so as to not look too related to their parents. Her kids never tried pulling tricks like that. They stuck by her side or ran off completely. Usually, they all stuck together since Maxine and Scott were their best friends. The Strackes were out in the crowd somewhere.

Before she could spot them, a smell like a dead ferret stuffed with lavender assaulted her nose. Ryan's own nose scrunched slightly, her smile gone, eyes widened.

Suzanne.

She glanced quickly at May who gave a quick nod, giving the silent permission Ryan needed before it was too late.

"May!" Suzanne hobbled toward them. "How are we doing on this fine morning?"

"Max?" Ryan turned and fled as quickly as she could without actually running away. "What have you been up to?"

"I am doing quite well," May said, stepping in between the sight of her fleeing daughter's figure and the over-zealous Suzanne. "How about yourself?"

"Absolutely blessed, dear. Blessed."

"What do you think of Father Green?" May asked. Maybe they could stick to small talk until Chris finished speaking with the father.

"He has potential. He seemed to have some . . . unique ideas when we last spoke. The father wanted to make a contemporary service, but I told him we are a traditional church." She nodded her head in emphasis. Her feathered hat bobbed with her like a stadium wave supporting her opinion. "And going to the youth is the wrong way to go."

"Really?" May asked. So much for keeping to small talk.

"Changes the church." She shook her head, the large nest of twisting cloth and feathers swayed against gravity. "The youth need to come to us, not the other way around."

"Hmm."

Suzanne was completely wrong, but it wasn't worth getting into. Not with her. It would probably be a good idea to make sure Father Green knew Suzanne spoke for only a small minority of the church, though. He should have been told that before Father Lee left, but she should make sure.

Elizabeth came to her rescue, thank you God, before Suzanne forced her to say anything more.

"Good morning, May. Suzanne."

"Always a pleasure, dearie," Suzanne said. "We were just talking about the youth of the church."

Elizabeth glanced at May. Her look was apologetic. Elizabeth must have thought she could get to her in time to prevent such a conversation. But now that Elizabeth was with her, they could shift the conversation away from how *the youth have corrupted the church* and other such topics.

"While I can't speak for him," May said, "I know Chris enjoys the services."

"How is Chris doing?" Elizabeth asked. "I don't think I've seen him since school let out."

And easy as that, the conversation swung away from church polity.

"He's doing well. Thank you for asking."

"Really?" Suzanne scoffed. "I would have said he's doing quite poor."

"Excuse me?" Both women turned to the crooning hat. She couldn't know about Chris. Elizabeth didn't even know.

"You should not hide such things, dearie. If they aren't talking about it now, they all will next week."

Elizabeth jumped to Chris's defense. "What are you talking about?"

"My son is fine." It couldn't be *that*, so what was she going on about?

"Then why is he speaking with the father?" Suzanne asked. May couldn't help but shudder a little at that woman's imitation of a warm smile. Decaying teeth stuck out in uneven rows. A terrible woman all the way through.

"That's none of your business," Elizabeth said.

"The health of this church is my business. One addict will only make more."

"Suzanne!"

Addict? She thought Chris was an addict? Who did she think she was?

May's hand was in a fist. Suzanne pursed her lips in a smug smile, her head tilted just enough to the side to show she believed everyone else thought so too. She was going to hit her. She really was.

"If you ever accuse my children of using again, I will take that dead bird you call a hat and shove it so far down your throat you'll be coughing up feathers all year."

Suzanne gasped and laid a hand over her chest as if her heart was too delicate for such words. May turned and stormed away. If that elitist crone said anything else she'd end up making good on her threat.

Those around her made a path for her to go through. Everyone in the room had probably heard her outburst, but no one cared. One couple smiled at her as she passed. They all knew Suzanne and knew she had done something to deserve it. They almost certainly had wanted to say the same to her at one point or another.

There was a small break in the crowd near the restrooms. She could wait for Chris to come out there. Keep an eye on the church doors. Elizabeth was right behind her when she stopped.

"They're not on drugs."

"I know," May seethed.

"Suzanne was just being . . ."

"Herself?" That did not make it any better. Chris was not using, but would Suzanne have said anything different if she knew the truth? Chris was heading down a bad path, and they could not hide his trouble from the rest of the church forever. If Father Green couldn't help him today. . .

"I was going to say 'bitch,'" Elizabeth said with a smile. "But yes. You know how she gets when people aren't paying attention to her. Father Green has the spotlight for now, so she's just trying to get everyone all riled up."

May's phone buzzed. Chris? She pulled it out, the tension in her chest breaking. Just a text from Scott:

Dont listen to that bitch

Chris isnt on drugs

May showed Elizabeth the phone and laughed, trying to force herself to relax. Chris would be fine.

"Like mother like son."

Her phone buzzed again:

Sry for cursing

Please dont tell mom

A little late for that.

Ryan, Scott, and Maxine worked their way through the crowd.

"Can we go to Egg and I?" Scott asked.

"After Chris gets out," Maxine added.

May peeled her eyes from the church doors. The kids were all smiles. Happy like they didn't know what Chris suffered. Did they know? She hadn't told Ryan to keep it a secret, but surely she would have known to keep family business to themselves. At least until after today.

Maxine said something else. Everyone laughed, so she smiled. Would things be the same if they knew? Elizabeth . . . she would support her, wouldn't she? Elizabeth was her best friend, her go-to-girl for advice, had been ever since Cesar. But this was different.

The church doors remained shut. Whatever the father was telling Chris, it was taking some time. But that was good. It meant he was getting the help he needed. Support, guidance, all the things a priest could offer.

When those doors finally opened, he'd keep getting that support. Whether that support came from good pancakes or anything else—he'd have it.

"May?" Elizabeth nudged her.

She jolted back to the conversation. "Oh, yes. Sorry. That works for us too."

"Alrighty then. Once Chris gets done, we'll—"

The church doors finally opened. Chris and Father Green stepped outside. Her sweetie smiled. The father put a hand on his shoulder and said something. Chris nodded. Everything else melted away. He was okay. Every last bit of tension drained out of her. Her breath filled her lungs with a comforting warmth.

"—speak of the devil."

"Ready for pancakes?" May asked. They could talk about his visit with Father Green on the way over. God willing, that would be the end of everything.

"Egg and I?" Chris asked.

"Where else?"

Chris didn't say anything as they parted from the Strackes and went to the car. He didn't speak at all, even after he buckled himself in. Just looked out the window toward the church.

May's hands were cold against the steering wheel. They had to talk. If he wasn't going to start, then she'd have to. That didn't make it any easier to get her mouth to open or for the air to uncoil from her chest so that she could actually say something. Anything.

"How'd everything go?"

Chris leaned against the window. His forehead smudged the glass.

"Pretty good," he said, pausing. Then, "We talked about his personal experiences with . . . gay people. Then he showed me some Bible verses."

"And?" May asked.

That answer didn't dismiss her worries. He'd been calm when he spoke: voice quiet and even. His expression wasn't hinting toward his feelings either. His reflection just barely visible in the window: not smiling, but not scowling. Eyes trained forward.

"He, he umm . . ."

May pulled out of the spot as Chris trailed off. She'd distracted him. Probably thrown off his train of thought by moving the car.

She had to get him talking again. Find something to comment on. It didn't have to be about church or the father. Just something to share between them.

"He also gave me some advice," Chris said, before she could speak. "He, Father Green, said I shouldn't keep you out of things. He says I should have told you what I was thinking sooner, and I know I haven't been very talkative lately, so . . . I'm, I'm sorry for that."

May smiled. Hearing that sent warm tingles along her arms. The knot in her chest vanished. Everything would be okay. Sure, he was avoiding the question in part, but he was showing he was fine while doing it. He probably didn't want her to worry about him. If she wasn't driving, she would have hugged Chris right then and there. Instead, she'd have to wait.

"I'm hugging you for that."

"What?"

"As soon as we stop. I'm coming right over and hugging you for saying that."

"Wait, but . . ."

"Ha-ha!" Ryan smiled before singing, "You're getting a hu-ug."

"What are you, six?" Chris grumbled, sliding lower in his seat.

May couldn't keep a smile off her face. How long had it been since they joked like this? "Keep it up and you'll get a hug too, missy."

Ryan gasped, but it was the fakest sound of distress May had ever heard, "On no, not a hug! Whatever will I do?"

"Hey, he's a teenage boy. Hugs from Mom are supposed to be terrible. You know how that works."

Chris's bravado slipped, and he let a smile crack along his lips.

"There's that smile." May laughed. That smile said more than anything else: he was okay. "Way too long since I've seen it."

Chris turned to face her and opened his mouth in a wide, toothy grin.

"Exactly," May said. "That's what I've been missing."

Chris rolled his eyes, but his smile faltered and slipped away completely. No, it could not be gone so soon. She had to get him to smile again, to keep things back the way they were.

"So, what have you been doing this last week?" May asked. They needed to keep the conversation going. Talking was the only way for all this to return to the way it was. He could not stop talking to her. Not again.

"Talking with Scott mostly," he said.

"Think you guys will meet up sometime this week?" May asked.

She glanced from the road toward Chris. He needed to get out of the house. That would help him clear Lisa's bad influence out of his head. He needed space to come out of this breakup, space away from the house and her. Chris didn't need her at the moment; as much as she wanted to help, he needed time with friends who could tell him "Lisa's a cheat." And he needed time with Scott, who would comment on the cute waitress, something May could never do with him.

"Yeah, umm . . . Anthony, his friend, actually invited us to go running with him in the morning. It would be before work."

"Really?" Chris had never been much for athletics, but maybe this change was what he needed.

Chris nodded. "I was going to ask you about it tonight."

"Where would you go?"

"Josephine Park."

Josephine Park was just a few streets down from St. Peters. They used to go there on weekends. A great place for families to spend a morning or afternoon. The city-planner's wife, Josephine, had pushed the mayor to set aside some land for local families. After a year of pestering him, the mayor had relented and told Josephine if she could raise the money she could have the land. Fundraising ended two months later and the park was named after her.

Ever since then, families from all over the city had come to the park which had become the perfect getaway from the suburb and the ghetto alike. A good place to run too: safe, well lit, and large enough to not be overly crowded. A good mix of people went there too. Couple of boys running around shouldn't have any trouble.

"What time would you need to be out of the house?" May asked.

"Six forty-five. I'll take the seven o'clock bus to the park."

"Alright. If you can get yourself up that early, you can go."

"Thanks, Mom."

"Hey, if it gets you out of the house," May laughed, turning into the Egg and I.

She couldn't jinx it by saying anything, but maybe this Anthony would be a big help in getting Chris to forget about Lisa.

Chris texted Monday morning to ask if the morning runs with Scott and Anthony could become a daily thing. It must have gone well then. May said yes, of course. She'd been trying to get Chris outside for years, so it would be a tad hypocritical to say no to running.

Especially considering how much it was clearly helping him. He came back from St. Peter's smiling like he'd done before Lisa. He even wandered in to chat before heading upstairs to his room.

"Hey, Mom. What are you working on?"

She looked up from her emails. There weren't many he'd be interested in. One from a single father asking about taking a promotion: night manager. It'd pay better, but he'd have less time to spend with his son—high school-aged—so there wasn't as much of a neglect angle to write.

"Just going through column requests." She'd tell them about the single father if there weren't any better ones by dinner. "How was the run?"

"Great. We went around the park twice." He smiled as he said that, clearly proud. And for good reason too. Two laps around Josephine Park had to be at least a few miles.

"You're not sore or anything?"

"Nah." He sat on the edge of her desk. "Well, maybe a little, but I like it."

May laughed, "Great to hear, sweetie. Maybe you can get Ryan running with you too someday."

His face went a little red at that. It was just the older brother thing to do, but really, how could he be embarrassed by Ryan? And besides, she would never agree to go running with him. That was just the little sister thing to do too.

"I'm not saying you have to now," May assured him. "But maybe if she wants to . . ."

He rolled his eyes. "I know, I know. I guess we can take her. Once. Someday."

"Alright," May smiled. "And work went alright?"

"Yeah, Father Green and I just got everything organized for Wednesday. Tomorrow we'll put up the decorations. Oh . . ." Chris hesitated. He looked away from her for a moment, but didn't keep his eyes trained on the floor like he'd done last week. Good: a sign of progress. "Father said he wanted to speak with you—if he could. Right after work would work for him, or during if that works better for you."

"Oh." She should have expected that. Of course he would want to speak with her about Chris. That first meeting may have been enough to stabilize Chris, but he needed consistent help to bring him out of this; to keep him on the right path moving forward. "Sure, how about I head over a few minutes before you get off. That way we can go out to lunch afterward?"

"Yeah." He smiled at her. Smiled! How was it something as simple as that could make her day? "That works for me."

Chapter 4

Daggers Drawn

DRIVING UP TO ST. Peter's on a weekday always made her feel like a kid again. How weird, considering the first time she had ever gone to a church was when she was pregnant with Chris, but she had the feeling then too. She'd been so meager compared with everything about the building: the steeple forced her to look up at the towering cross, the stained glass shaped the light, even the simple fact that the whole building was a gathering place for God. Everything was better than her. All the good Catholics inside seemed to have their lives together. They knew what they were doing. They were saved! But she'd just been some knocked up teen. . .

Sometimes, it was good to feel like a kid again. Like whenever she was coming up to see something Chris or Ryan had done, or if she was picking them up for something. On those days, that small feeling reminded her how lucky she was to have kept the kids. But some days it would have been nice to feel big, like an adult in charge of her life, as she came up to and passed through those doors.

There wasn't a reason for her to be worried about the upcoming meeting. Father Green was helping Chris, but she couldn't shake that old feeling of trudging to her principal for something she and Cesar had done. That feeling all but vanished when she climbed out of the car. Father Green and Chris were hanging up a banner for tomorrow. The two of them were wearing almost the same thing. Like Chris, Father Green had on a mission trip t-shirt and basketball shorts.

Shorts? May stared at him as she approached. Father Lee would never have worn anything as flashy as those teal shorts. He would probably have worn a button-down and khaki shorts, if not jeans. But it was a hot day and Father Green was working outside. He was also younger than their old father. Chris thought he was cooler too; maybe wearing shorts while working outside contributed to that.

Chris and Father Green stepped back from the banner. It held up by itself, straight and ready to welcome the kids. Father Green held up his hand, closed in a fist toward Chris who bumped it. Neither of them turned from the banner as they did. Clearly, they were proud of their work. When Chris did look away from the banner, he was smiling. His whole face lit up.

"Looks good, sweetie," May said.

Chris turned. "Hey, Mom."

"May." Father took a step toward her, hand outstretched. "Great to be able to talk."

She shook it. "Likewise."

Likewise? That was far too formal for this. She was starting to sound just like Suzanne. First, you're thinking about how the father's improper for wearing shorts, next you're accusing people of selling drugs.

"Chris, I'll talk with May inside. Can you gather up everything and put it in the youth room?"

"Sure thing," Chris nodded.

"Alright, May. Let's head back to my office."

He opened the door. The walls were covered in green poster paper. The kids were going to love this. The tops had been cut into strips to look like grass. A few large papier-mâché buffalo heads and shoulders even peeked out from around the corner at the end of the hall.

"I hope you don't mind doing some organizing while we talk," Father Green said. "My office is absolutely filled with papers."

"Oh." They weren't going to just sit for this meeting? That was certainly strange. Unorthodox at the very least. "That will be fine."

Maybe Father Green had some reason behind doing this. It might be intended to take her mind off of things, or help her to relax as this was a big deal. He might just be scatterbrained or in need of catching up with everything coming to a new church brought.

He opened the door to his office. It seemed like the latter reason was right. "Filled with papers" would have been an understatement—there wasn't an inch of his desk that wasn't covered. There were even stacks of papers on his bookshelf, and the books themselves were stacked up in little towers beside the shelves.

May stared at the two chairs in the office, both on their side of the desk, and both had a handful of colored folders on them. This was certainly going to be an unorthodox meeting.

"We just need one of each paper in the folders," he explained, picking up one stack of folders before he sat down. "They're for the parents tomorrow morning."

May took the seat across from him.

"Chris is a big help around here," Father Green said. "I can't imagine getting all this done without him. It's hard to believe we got it all done just the two of us ourselves. I don't mean to disparage Father Lee's decisions, but it seems like it'd be much easier to have all volunteers start the week on Monday. Having them come into the mix along with the kids just seems messy, but we'll see . . ."

"Chris has said the same thing," May said.

If only he'd get on with it, skip to the part where he would tell her everything would be fine, but she couldn't. He was a priest, after all. It wouldn't just be rude to do that, it would probably mess up whatever he had planned for her this meeting. He trusted God, and she trusted God's judgment as well as the father's, so she just had to wait and follow what they laid out. Knowing that didn't make this any easier.

She finished three folders before he said anything else. "You're the only single mother here, you know? I hope we're inclusive, but Chris is the only LatinX person around here and I'm the only black man too. Why do you think that is?"

May opened her mouth to speak but stopped mid-breath. How was she supposed to answer that?

The father waved the thought away. "That's for another time. Maybe related, maybe not, but . . . in any case. Chris told me he thinks he's gay."

She tucked the last paper into the plastic folder and swallowed back the choking lump of dread in her throat. There it was. How did hearing it from him make it so much worse? More real? It was something outside of their family now. What was he going to say? What had he said back when they first met? An issue for another time. For now. What had kept him from saying anything then?

"What do you think about that?" he asked. "About him telling you he's gay?"

May had always felt like a kid in this room. Father Lee had held her intervention from right there where Father Green now sat. In this same room she'd heard about Henry and Stephanie's accident; felt the blood leave her face as she realized Ryan was now her legal daughter. That moment only changed one word, but everything changed with it too. From that day, she'd become a single mother. And it had all started right here.

"What do you mean?" Surely it was wrong. Lust was always wrong: one of the seven deadly sins. Of course she would be against him telling her that.

"What do you think about homosexuality?"

He wanted her to say it, to affirm what needed to be done. But what needed to be done?

"It's wrong."

"Why?" he closed the folder he'd been working on and looked at her. Stared at her in the way only a priest could. That look held every part of her attention; it didn't matter if he was dressed like a high schooler or not.

"Why is it wrong?" Did he want her to explain it to him? Maybe he just wanted to help her find the words for a later conversation with Chris.

Father Green nodded. He didn't say anything else, only kept nodding. His eyes never left her while he did, either. They kept boring into her own. She couldn't concentrate, it was impossible for her to think straight.

"It's a sin," she said. But he wanted more than that, didn't he? He wanted her to explain why it was a sin. Chris would need her to be able to do that. "It's sex outside of marriage. Lust."

"What if Chris were to marry a man?" Father Green said it with an even voice. His calm, rigid face hardly moved or showed her any sign of what he meant. "Would same-sex behavior be wrong in that case?"

"Yes," May said.

The father said nothing in return. She had to say more, explain why again. She closed her eyes and leaned back. It was a sin of lust. Acting gay was close to being the same sin she had done with Cesar. Only with another man there was no chance of God slipping in a broken condom for redemption. Nothing good could be found in that sin. She kept her eyes closed for only a second, but that was all she needed. "It's sex without purpose. Sex without the chance of kids is just for yourself."

Father Green looked away behind her and nodded; a few slow, small tips of his head, as though thinking over what she had said. He stood, turning his back to her as he reached out to his bookcase. His hand brushed along the book spines.

"Do you know my favorite part about Christianity?" he did not turn around to ask her that. "On the surface, it's black and white. Everything is," he continued without waiting for a response. "You have God and evil. Jesus and death. But when you bury yourself in the text, you can find a lot of gray in there too. Verses that some call contradictions or mistakes."

He stopped scanning his shelves and slipped out a book. "Take sex," he said turning to her. "You said it was for procreation. If I asked everyone at Mass one day, I'd probably get that same answer. But putting sex into that small of a box forgets Scripture."

She took the book from his hands. *Contemporary Exegesis: Sex in the Bible.*

"This is a collection of essays about sex."

She would have blushed if she weren't so shocked by the turn of this conversation. Was the father saying homosexuality was fine?

"In proper relationships, sex can be an almost holy act. There's a reason God made it good, after all."

He smiled then, the first time since they'd walked in. "But there's where we come into the gray of it. What does it mean to be in a proper relationship? This book does its best to answer that, but . . ." He took his seat again and set the book down on the desk beside them. "In any case, take the book with you and read it. But you didn't come here to just talk about the definitions of love and proper relationships. We're here for Chris. Understanding the role of sex is something we must talk about, but it is not the only thing . . . not the most important thing.

"Do you know what Chris told me he was most afraid of when he talked with me last Sunday?"

"No." May's answer was a whisper. Chris had avoided her all week. He stayed away from her. He hid his tears, made sure Ryan was in the room whenever he had to see her. He was afraid of her. Of what she would do when he told her.

"He didn't know what you would say."

"I . . ."

May had gone to an amusement park once in her life. Cesar took her out to one on a date. They waited an hour to ride the tallest rollercoaster there. Both of them were excited at first, but as they stepped closer and closer, the massive drops became larger and her anticipation vanished. Instead, she started wanting to back up in line. She couldn't of course, she always had to move forward with the line, her feet getting heavier like they were sinking in mud, until she was standing right there at the metal gate. She couldn't pick up her feet then. She could hardly move at all then. Could hardly move any better now.

"He thought you'd hate him."

Something caught in her throat. She swallowed. Hard, but the lump stayed stuck—made it hard to breathe. None of the father's smile remained. He stared at her with those priestly eyes, as if condemning her for her inability to save Chris. For letting him get to that point of darkness in the first place. For failing as a mother.

"I couldn't—"

"—and you don't, but did you ask yourself why it took him so long to come to you about this? He couldn't trust you to love him, and that May . . . that's the worst of all this. He was scared and he couldn't come to you about it."

"He could." The lump melted in her throat. How could her sweetie think that? She'd be there for anything. Shouldn't matter what went wrong —didn't matter.

"But he didn't know! He didn't and you almost lost him for that." Father Green tilted his head down so he looked at the desk. He breathed a loud, solid breath filling the space between them. "You can't ever let him think that again. Because if he thinks, even for a moment that you've given up on him, you'll lose him, May. And that's something, more than anything else, that we cannot allow to happen."

May and Chris watched the church door close. With the father back inside, they turned to leave.

"Sooo . . ." Chris said, hands in pockets.

May continued toward the car and took a deep breath. He probably wanted to know what she and the father had talked about, but what could she say when there were so many things that needed to be said first?

She would never leave him. He could come to her with anything. They were going to get through this. No matter what it took, they would get through this.

"I love you."

That was the most important thing. Above all the struggles Chris had ahead of him, he needed to know that. She loved him. Now and forever.

"Mom—"

"How could you think I'd leave you?"

He froze and stared at her. His whole back turned rigid, but his expression was open,wide, like she'd cussed at him.

Wooziness overcame her, her legs seemed to shake, but she stayed upright. Why couldn't they be sitting for this? She could have delayed until they were in the car. Waited until tomorrow, pushed it back to another day, left it to be forgotten behind them in the start of the new school year.

"I didn't." He closed his eyes. For a long moment, he let out a breath. Tense shoulders relaxed and slumped. He opened his eyes again, showing them to be wet. They shook as he looked at her. As if they were swimming, maybe searching for something; maybe the words she couldn't find to put all this to bed. "I . . . didn't know what you'd say. I thought—I'd heard of parents kicking out their kids, sending them to these camps."

"Sweetie . . ."

Saying the word took all her breath. Did Chris really think she would give up on him so easily? After everything they'd been through to keep them together. Would he give up on *her*? On the life they'd struggled to have, for something as simple as lust?

He laughed: just a short, little burst of air through his nose, but an honest-to-goodness laugh. And thank God, he even smiled! The tears in his eyes didn't go away, but there was a smile.

"I know." He looked down toward her feet, but that slight grin stayed on his face. The tension gripping her legs vanished. He was smiling.

"I love you too."

May opened her arms: everything would be okay. "Come here, sweetie."

She pulled Chris closer, her head pressed against his shoulder. He remained stiff, as though he didn't know how to hug his mother back. But that didn't last long. Finally, he wrapped his own arms around her.

She held onto his arms for a moment longer when they separated. Chris's eyes were a little red, but aside from that small, persisting tinge, the tears had vanished. He smiled, eyes glancing away from hers to the ground.

"It's going to be like this all Thursday, isn't it?" he asked.

"Thursday?" She'd forgotten in all of last week's commotion. Maxine was moving away on Saturday. "The going away party."

"Yeah." Chris nodded and she dropped her arms from his.

"You and Scott will be the only dry eyes around."

How nice to cry about something else for a change. Maxine's departure would give them all a much-needed distraction for the next week. That would get them through to Sunday. Then, Father Green could answer all the questions he hadn't touched on today.

"She's only moving two hours away."

"That doesn't mean her leaving will be any easier, you know. There's a big difference between living down the hall and down the interstate."

Heaven knew it would be hard on her. Chris's own leaving was coming up faster than she'd like. A year from now, and he'd be packing for college. And he'd already said he wouldn't be staying in town for undergrad like Maxine had done.

"Yeah, I guess."

"You *guess*?"

"I mean, we all have to leave at some point though, right?"

"Sweetie, I'm not ever letting you leave," May laughed.

Chris rolled his eyes, "Don't even joke about that."

"I know, I know. You can't wait to get out of here."

Chris hesitated. No smile in that pause, either. He just quietly looked away from her like he was hiding something; as if guilty of the thought.

May stared at the dark reflection of her face on the computer. A whole half hour sitting there and she hadn't even reached out to turn on the monitor. She closed her eyes. The last two nights had been . . . better. Maxine's party on Thursday took most of their attention off of everything, and then there had been the gig last night.

The days were the problem.

Chris didn't sit down when he had talked with her. He had stood at the end of the room, leaning up against the wall where he could slip away at any second. He had kept looking down to the book, the one from Father Green, the one they never talked about. The few times she had started to mention it, he'd pressed himself back into the wall like he wanted to run away.

A subtle enough display; he was just as uncomfortable with this as she was. If only they could forget the whole episode and move on with their lives. Planning for Maxine's going away party had helped, but she was gone now. She'd left this morning.

She could serve as a distraction for a few more days. They could talk about how he, Ryan, Scott, and Maxine used to play together, or about how Maxine used to babysit for her whenever she and the Strackes wanted a night away from the kids. They could even talk about how weird it was that all the kids got along so well. The six-year age difference between Ryan and Maxine never seemed to bother them.

As nice as Ryan was, she couldn't get the credit for that. It was all Maxine. She was always able to keep all the kids entertained. She never left out Ryan. She could make dirt fun if she tried, that's how good she was about it all.

She'd have been able to keep Chris smiling too.

Something moved outside. May just caught a glance of it out through the window. Was that Elizabeth? What was she doing out there? They weren't supposed to work on the garden until it had cooled off some.

Elizabeth knelt in the garden, her hands were already covered in dirt from pulling at the scattered weeds. She was going to give herself heatstroke, working in the sun like that. May hurried into the kitchen and poured two glasses of water. She opened the door and called to Elizabeth, "You do realize this is the hottest part of the day, right?"

Elizabeth wiped at her sweating brow and squinted against the bright light to look at May. May could see her red-tinged eyes through the almost-closed lids.

"Have you been weeding?"

May shook her head. She'd forgotten, but she had been watering.

Elizabeth scowled down at the beds, "You need to remember to weed. Not weeding will kill a garden as fast as any rabbit."

"I brought you some water." May offered the glass. Elizabeth must have been out here to keep her mind busy, but there were better ways of doing that than gardening in hundred-degree weather.

Elizabeth looked around the garden, seemingly satisfied with her progress. Or maybe she knew what May was trying to do.

"You want to cool off inside for a little bit?" May asked.

"Thank you." Elizabeth stood. She smiled as she rose, just a small move, but enough. May could repay Elizabeth today for all she'd done, help distract her in the same way Maxine's departure had helped her through the last week.

The poor woman needs cool air, May thought, leading the way to the living room. Elizabeth practically collapsed onto the couch and was halfway through her water before May joined her on the other end.

"I know I still have Scott," Elizabeth said. "But I can't help feeling like I already have an empty nest."

May nodded. "I don't know what I'll do when Chris leaves next year. There'll be half the laundry, half the dishes—"

"—half the random messes to pick up."

"None of those left for me. Ryan's practically a ghost here. She never leaves anything out of place."

"I always wished Maxine would pick up Ryan's cleanliness," she sighed. "But maybe she'll be cleaner when she comes back."

"Give it a month. Maxine will be back with trash bags full of laundry and a stomach hungry for a good meal."

"Scott said the same thing last night," Elizabeth said. "He picked up a piece of cornbread and shook it at Maxine, *sure you won't miss this?*"

May frowned. That didn't make sense. Chris ate with Scott and Anthony before the concert last night. Surely, Scott didn't eat twice. Or maybe the Stracke family had an early dinner and Scott hadn't ordered anything with the boys.

Elizabeth noticed her concern. "May? Is everything alright?"

"Chris said he went out with Scott last night. Before the concert."

"Oh. May, Scott stayed at the house until he had to leave for the sound check."

May couldn't open her mouth to speak. Why would Chris lie to her? What happened to being not keeping each other out of things? He had to be hiding something, but what?

"I'm sure it's nothing, May. He probably met someone else for dinner before the concert."

"Why wouldn't he tell me that, though?"

Suzanne's accusations came back to her. No. No—he could not be on drugs. He would not. Not her son. Chris knew what they could do to him, what they would do to him, and he most *certainly* knew what she would do to him.

"Maybe he didn't think you'd let him meet someone else. Do you think he could have gone to seen Lisa?"

Did he do something with a boy? With Anthony? No, Chris couldn't —he wouldn't. They were making progress. He was getting better, though they could have done more. Father Green should have brought them all together. They should have sat down with Chris and gone over everything, shown him it was wrong.

May forced herself to swallow a sip of water. She couldn't tell Elizabeth about that—about what Chris could have been doing. "No," she sounded hoarse. "No, I think that ship's sailed between them."

That small line sounded weak, but Elizabeth laughed anyway. She was a good friend like that. She would be able to help with Chris, wouldn't she? Distract her, at the very least. Give her the same small jokes and talks she was receiving now. Anything to keep their minds off the all pressing concern for the kids.

The staircase echoed with the pounding of Chris's footsteps. He swung around the bannister and half-ran into the living room. He saw Elizabeth and stopped short.

"Hey, Mrs. Stracke."

"Good afternoon, Chris." Elizabeth stood and looked back down to May. "I'm going to finish up in the garden."

She set her glass down on the living room table. May nodded. "I'll be out there soon."

May took a deep breath. How would she confront him? She could not drive him away. Not that it was true. It wasn't true. It couldn't be. Because it wasn't true, and because he should never fear coming to her about anything, she had to be careful about how she phrased this conversation.

"I was just going to get a drink," Chris said. "I didn't mean to interrupt or anything."

"Where were you last night?"

Chris's pupils dilated—a little. The way he always did when he'd been caught.

"Dinner then the concert. Why?"

This boy. He was going to make her say it—accuse him of lying to her. "Who did you go with?"

"Anthony. Scott had to cancel." He said it plain, simple, like he didn't have anything to hide. His eyes didn't change. Had they changed at all? They had to have. There was that dilation. There was. He was hiding something.

"Is Anthony gay?"

"What? No, no, he's . . ." Chris sighed. He looked away from her, toward the couch. "I wanted him to be—when I first met him. He's . . . he's sort of the reason I came out to you."

The tension melted off May's shoulders. Her whole body relaxed, every knot from her back to those in her gut and throat went away. She was being a fool. Her stomach unclenched and she realized she'd been holding her breath. But she couldn't relax. He wasn't lying to her, but what did this all mean? If Anthony were straight, why would he tell Chris he was gay? Or, did he encourage Chris to talk with her about all this?

"I saw him and . . ." He continued, his eyes fixed on the couch. Half his face was hidden, but he was smiling. "I liked him right off the bat. More than I've liked anyone . . . any girl." His face rushed red and he shifted, hiding his face entirely from her. "I can't . . . it wasn't . . . it's not love. But it's something I never felt for Lisa. And I'd been thinking about things for a while and I just sort of told him. Asked him out I guess. He said no."

Chris shook his head and made a noise that sounded like a snort, or sniffle, as if he were laughing at himself. "Not . . ." Chris turned back to face her.

He was smiling. A full smile too! But it was Anthony that made him smile. Was it a smile like those he had around Scott or one like with Lisa?

"He told me I had to tell you what I was thinking."

"He did?" How did this boy, this stranger, do more for Chris than she could have? She hadn't even known anything was wrong. How could she have known without Chris telling her? And now, this boy had turned him back to her.

"I think you'd like him," he added.

"If this keeps up we'll never know will we?" May laughed. Anthony had become a close friend it seemed, the two boys hung out all the time, but she'd never seen him. He'd done so much for them but she couldn't even say what he looked like.

"What's that supposed to mean?" Chris laughed.

"You two have hung out every day, but I hardly know anything about him."

"I haven't even known him for a month!"

"So is that when I'll get to meet him? Why don't you invite him over for dinner sometime next week?"

"Al—alright," Chris said. A smile spread along his face, "I'll text him."

"Good," May stood. "Now, I'm going to help Elizabeth finish in the garden. When we're done, I expect an answer." Chris nodded. "Then, the two of us are going figure out what's for dinner and you can tell me all about Anthony while we cook."

"Hey, Mom?" May stopped, she turned in the doorway to look back at him. Chris held his phone in his hands, phone in his hands, eyes up and looking right at her instead of the screen. His smile had only grown wider.

"I love you."

Chapter 5

Still Young

"HE PLAYS IN THE Jasper marching band," Chris said. He was telling her about Anthony as they made dinner. So far, he was right. She did like the boy. At least, she liked what she knew about him.

"That's how he became Max's replacement in the band," he continued. "Oh, and he does parkour."

"Parkour?"

"Yeah. Free running."

"Oh, so what the two of you do in the park?"

"No, that's just running. Parkour's like extreme running. Going up fences and buildings and things."

"Really? Do you think you're going to try it out?"

"No," he laughed. "Not yet at least."

"Well . . . " she turned her head to think. If he only did it during the day with Anthony or Scott it should be fine. Elizabeth would definitely disapprove, but: "If you ever wanted to, you'd have my support."

"Really?"

She nodded. "But no fences. Don't want anyone getting any ideas. And nothing higher than five feet off the ground."

Chris shook his head and laughed again. Funny how just a short while ago she was afraid she'd never hear that sound again. And yet here he was, back as if he'd never dated Lisa. Goodness, she was starting to become a tired record. Maybe meeting Anthony would help clear her mind of those same, old thoughts.

"What do the two of you talk about?"

"We mainly talk about music and—uhh, school stuff."

"School stuff?" she shot him a look. As if she'd buy that. He was lying to her now—hiding something at least. But this didn't seem like anything big. Just something to joke about, or something she wouldn't like. But that didn't mean it was anything wrong. "What *school stuff* do you have to talk about in June?"

"You know. College, and old gossip . . ."

"Uh-huh."

Chris set the bowl of cranberry sauce aside and started cleaning the carrots for steaming.

"We also talk about religion some."

"Oh?" That was surprising. Evangelizing was never something she'd encouraged, but that was mainly because she had to tell her story so often. No reason he couldn't do it if he wanted.

"What does he believe—if I can ask?"

"He doesn't know." Chris paused, seemingly trying to summarize many conversations down to a sentence or two. "He likes a lot of what I've told him about the church: Love your neighbor, be good, yadda-yadda-yadda, all the main things, but he doesn't agree with some of the teachings."

"Like what?"

"Uhh, the . . . big one is . . . homosexuality."

"Oh." It made sense for them to have talked about that. After all, Chris had said he'd wanted the boy to be gay. They'd probably talked about it that first night. Must have. Anthony had told Chris to talk with her after all.

May frowned. It was hard to keep everything straight. What did that mean Anthony believed? He could have known it was a sin, but he also could have thought Chris just needed to be honest with her.

"What does he think about it?" Just asking that made something tighten in her chest; like she was up on a high rope, but this conversation was safer than any other they'd had about it. Yet, despite that, the knot still lingered. That thing keeping her from saying *it*.

"He, umm . . ." Chris brought the carrots over to the wooden cutting board and started cutting them into thin, circular pieces. "He thinks it's a tad hypocritical for a church to preach love while discriminating."

"The church discriminates against the sin," May explained, even though Chris surely knew that. "It's the action that's wrong. Not the person."

"Why is it wrong? He asked me," Chris added quickly. "And I'll admit I don't know enough to answer him. Anthony says so long as it's between two consenting adults, it doesn't hurt anyone."

May shook her head. That simply wasn't true. "It can do harm—it does do harm. Premarital sex almost ruined my life. You are the one good thing to come from my desire, but homosexuals—they can't have that goodness in their lust. It just is not possible for them to have a child together. There's no hope of redemption in that sin."

Chris grunted, "Son of a—" He snapped his mouth shut as he gripped his hand. Blood glimmered on wood.

Oh God! Her hand shot toward him. Was he okay? A cut? How deep was it? Was his finger still attached?

"Chris! What—"

"—nicked myself with the knife," he said through clenched teeth.

"Ryan! Get the First-Aid kit!" May shouted and turned toward the stairs. Would Ryan have headphones on?

"It's fine. It's fine," Chris said, moving to the sink as he spoke. Ryan's footsteps thundered down the stairs. May ripped a handful of paper towels from their roll and tried to see the cut, "Let me see it."

She wiped the blood away. It wasn't long, or deep, thank God. No way was that going to stop her from fussing over him. May helped Chris keep pressure on the wound.

"What happened?" Ryan asked.

"He cut himself."

"The knife slipped."

"Get me a wipe and a Band-Aid," May said. "This might sting."

May took the wipe and cleaned the cut with it. Chris winced a little, but did not make any noise of complaint. Her little trooper.

Ryan opened the Band-Aid and handed it to May. She took it, peeling off the backing.

"Aw, not the Scooby ones," Chris groaned. "Can't I get the other ones?"

Yep; her little trooper.

"It'll be fine," May said. "You can pick out whichever you like if you need another one in the morning."

Chris's phone buzzed on the table. Before he could say anything, Ryan spun it around and read the text.

"It's from Anthony."

"Hey!"

"He wants to know if he should bring anything Tuesday."

May looked at the bloody carrots. Chris wouldn't be cutting any more of those for at least a week.

Ryan seemed to have the same thought. "I'll tell him some veggies."

May spent all of Tuesday afternoon watching Chris rush around the house. Apparently, everything had to look perfect for Anthony. He was always like that, wanting things cleaned up for visitors. Scott used to always joke Chris was the mom of their family, but he stopped doing that a few years ago when one of his old girlfriends heard him say that and went off on him about gender roles and *not being a masochistic swine-head.* Scott hadn't helped things by correcting her to *misogynistic,* but he never called Chris *Mamma Flowers* again, so everything worked out in the end.

Chris only stopped running around when the doorbell rang.

"I got it," May said, waving Chris back into the kitchen. Honestly, the boy wanted to do everything, but he'd just end up dropping the pie if she didn't tell him to relax.

Chris nodded and retreated into the kitchen.

May opened the door, revealing a boy. He was taller than her by a few inches, and stood up straight, but he probably only did that because he was just meeting her for the first time. One hand balanced a plastic Tupperware container while the other played with the collar of his button-down, but it quickly dropped to his side when the door squeaked.

"You must be Anthony." May ushered the boy inside and took the Tupperware from him. "Chris has told me so much about you."

"Only the boring things, I hope."

He stepped over the threshold and took in the room.

"He's saved the good stories for tonight, I'm sure." May smiled. "Let's bring those to the kitchen. Chris and Ryan should have everything ready."

"They didn't let you help?"

"Not tonight. Chris wanted it to be perfect, so I was left out of the kitchen."

"I thought you couldn't help because you had that post to write?" Ryan said, meeting them at the kitchen door.

"There was that too."

"Anthony!" Chris called from behind Ryan. "You made it."

"Dad dropped me off on his way to work."

"Oh?" May tried to enter the conversation. Where did his father work at this hour?

Anthony did not hear her, or he did not take her *oh* to be a question. He and Ryan entered the kitchen.

"Good work with the veggies," she laughed.

"Well, I didn't want Chris to be hurting himself again, did I?"

"Hey! I can make a Hachis Parmentier that'll put you into a food-coma, but you're going to make fun of me for cutting myself?"

"Yep," Anthony said.

"It's what we do."

"Well, then. The next time you want a soufflé, you'll just have to go to someone else."

"What?" May followed after the kids. "No soufflé! Kids, apologize this instant."

"You can relax, Mom. I'll still make it for you."

"Oh, well. Carry on then."

They laughed; all of them. Thank you, God. This night might go well. Maybe tonight she could find a way to repay Anthony for all he'd done.

May looked around the kitchen. Everything was ready: plates and utensils on the table with the food, four glasses out on the kitchen island waiting for them to put their drinks in.

"So, Ryan and I just get to watch you two eat soufflé tonight?"

"You can relax too, Anthony," May said. "Chris made a pie for us to share."

"It may not sound nearly as fancy," Ryan said. "but it's absolutely delicious."

"The trick is to not use store-bought dough," Chris explained. "After that it's pretty easy to make a good cherry pie."

"Cherry pie? You made me a cherry pie!" Anthony laughed and Chris pulled that wide smile he did whenever he'd done something that made him mischievously proud.

"What's wrong with cherry pie?" Ryan asked.

"Nothing."

"Doesn't look like nothing from his Cheshire smile," May pointed to Chris.

"It's a bit of a story," Chris explained.

"Would you be willing to share it?"

"How about while we eat," Ryan said. "I'm starving."

"Chris, would you like to say grace?" May asked.

They bowed their heads as Chris recited the short prayer. Anthony put his head down as well, but didn't look up when it was over, as if it took him a moment to realize the prayer was finished. How polite of him. You had to commend the boy on that. A lot of people found it uncomfortable to be around Catholics before a meal. Most just stared at their plate until she finished the sign of the cross, but Anthony had actually bowed his head. Respect like that would get him far in life.

"So, cherry pie?" Ryan asked, picking up the bowl of rice, and scooped some onto her plate.

"Oh, that." Chris blushed a little and started to serve himself.

Anthony rolled his eyes and began, "There was this couple in Josephine Park arguing about—"

"—something," Chris interjected.

"Something." Anthony nodded. "But they never said what. Instead whenever they were about to name whatever it was, one of them would get all quiet and do that loud shouting whisper thing, you know the one that angry people make when they are trying to not be overheard, and they would say *cherry pie* or make a *cherry pie.*"

"Any idea what cherry pie meant?" Ryan asked.

Chris and Anthony glanced at each other. Chris got red faced and looked down at his plate.

"Oh."

"Something not suitable for dinner conversation," Anthony said.

"So, drugs or sex?" Ryan asked.

"Ryan!" May said, but in all honesty she couldn't tell the difference between which it could be either.

"Sorry." Ryan smiled though. She probably wasn't trying to make trouble. It's more likely she wanted to give a good first impression of their family; show they were *cool.*

"Oh, it's alright," May sighed. So long as nobody went too far, jokes and language like that wouldn't be too bad. "Truth is I'm curious too."

Ryan's smile got a little wider and—did she just nod? Did that mean she was making a good first impression?

"Don't know," Anthony said. "They looked like they were a couple, but by the way they were arguing she could've been his dealer too."

"Which do you think they were?"

"I think they were a couple, but Chris thinks she's a dealer."

"They were sketchy-looking," Chris said.

"Okay, yeah, they were, but you don't go to Josephine Park for a drug deal. That's what Rude Street's for."

He was right on that point. Rude Street was her old neighborhood. When she'd left, it was nothing but crack house after crack house, and over the years it had not gotten better. Not that she'd ever set foot back in her childhood haunt, but it was an established fact: if you wanted to get high, you went to Rude.

"There aren't even any dealers on my street," he continued. "Why'd they go further up to the park?"

"Where do you live?" May asked.

"Mercer Boulevard."

May stifled a groan. That wasn't much better. Only a few streets down from Rude Street.

"Is that the street where that fight happened?" Ryan asked.

"Which one?"

"The one straight out of *The Outsiders*. Wasn't one of the gangs involved called the Greasers?"

Anthony shook his head. "I think I know who you're talking about, but they don't call themselves that. They're the Fratellos."

"Greasers is what they're called at St. Francis," Chris explained.

"Okay, so was the fight with the *Fratellos* on your street?"

"Sort of. It started between us and Rude, but most of them ended up getting arrested on our street."

"That's awful," Chris said.

Anthony shrugged, and May agreed. It's just how things were. Dealers sold and got busted on your doorstep, and pick-up games were broken apart by cops just as often as passing cars. Didn't make it right, but that's how it was. She'd been lucky to get out; hopefully Anthony would do the same. He played music, seemed smart too, and wasn't on drugs. He could get out. He could leave and never look back like May had done. But until then, nothing to do but wait it out.

Wait, no—no that wasn't true. She could help. She could provide him a lifeline if he ever needed it, offer encouragement and support when it came time for applications. And if the absolute worst were to happen, she could take him in. Just as Henry and Stephanie had cared for her, she could care for him.

Anthony set down his empty glass. "Can I get a refill?"

"Sure." The boy was very polite. He could just be on his absolute best behavior for her, or maybe he was always that respectful. Maybe Chris had been a good influence on the boy.

"Hey, Ms. Flowers, what's this?"

Anthony had stopped midway to the refrigerator; he stood, pointing at their curse jar. It used to be one of those small mason jars jam came in, but they'd cleaned it out and decorated it with flowers.

"Our curse jar."

"Is that why it says shit on it?"

They'd also put two curses. May sighed. How did he find it so quickly? She hadn't even found that one until Scott pointed out the small *damn* Ryan had written in herself. Chris and Ryan had each independently hidden swear words amid the flowers. They hid them pretty well too. Chris's *shit* lay between the petals of two daisies, while Ryan's *damn* curled around a rose stem. May hadn't notice either one for years. She probably never would have seen them if not for Scott.

"Pretty much," Ryan said.

He peered into the jar. "You guys must curse a lot."

"Other things go in there too."

"Like any loose change we find," Ryan said.

"Or if we get caught lying," Chris added. But they had to be big lies for that. Nothing like the little lie Chris had told the other day, trying to avoid talking about homosexuality.

"And any drugs are a ten-thousand-dollar charge."

Anthony blew out a low whistle. "And what do you guys do with the money?"

May smiled. "Family outings!"

"We're going to try Mrs. Asim's Brownie Town once the jar's filled."

"You need to curse more, then. Brownie Town's leaving soon."

"I asked Scott to text before they stop selling it. We'll just go with what we have if it's not filled by then."

Anthony dug out his wallet. May couldn't help but stare. It was a tattered old thing: one side held together entirely by duct-tape. What was he doing?

"No offense, but I'm going to try and avoid paying for your ice cream from now on." He slid out a dollar bill and stepped to the jar.

"You don't need to do that," May protested. "You didn't know."

"Rules are rules," Anthony insisted. "Not knowing about them doesn't mean I'm allowed to break them."

May smiled. Anthony was certainly doing a good job of making a first impression. Much better than Lisa, who'd muttered a curse under her breath for some slight—May still wasn't certain what. Ryan had made a joke about putting a dollar in the jar, and she'd gotten even more upset and ended up storming out of the house. She'd known then and there: Lisa was bad for Chris.

Anthony though, now he could be a good friend.

After filling their bellies with cherry pie and ice cream, they retired to the living room where the real conversation began.

"What instruments do you play?" May asked. Anthony had been pleasant during dinner, but he hadn't really said all that much about himself. Surely he played the trumpet, that was what Maxine played after all, but he probably played more than that. Most members of the band could play multiple instruments.

"Mostly French horn during the school year, but I do mellophone for marching band, and I picked up trumpet a few years ago when my band director needed a soloist."

"Wow." That was impressive. Skills like that could get the boy out of the slums and into college. After all, she could hardly carry a tune in the car, let alone play an instrument—or three!

"Once you can do one, it's not too hard to pick up the others."

Ryan rolled her eyes. "Ugh . . . prodigies."

May agreed with her on that. He'd said it as if playing multiple instruments were the easiest thing in the world. Maybe it was—to him. Maybe music came to him in the same way cooking came to Chris, or math to Ryan.

"Oh!" Chris sat up quickly. "That reminds me. I wanted to show you that poster I told you about."

He didn't need to say anymore for May to know exactly which one he was talking about. She'd given him the poster when he was eleven; he'd just won his first adult cooking contest. It was of a kid in a lab coat with a tall, shadowy figure behind him. The caption read: *Behind every prodigy is a prodding mother.* It would have been the perfect poster if the child were Chris, except it was of a girl with messy pigtails.

"Why don't you give him a tour of the house?" May said. "You can show him the poster while Ryan and I clean up."

"I can help," Anthony offered.

"Nonsense." May waved him off as she stood. "You're a guest tonight. You can help the next time you come over, but for now take a tour and relax."

"Really?" Anthony asked. He seemed surprised by her offer for him to return.

"Thanks, Mom. Come on, Anthony, we can start with my room."

May shook her head as the two boys went upstairs. It's like he was a kid again, showing off his room and toys.

"What do you think of him?" Ryan asked.

"Anthony?" May stood and headed to the kitchen as Ryan pulled out her phone, probably to put on The Cat Empire. They could talk and clean well enough while listening to the music. Lord knew it'd be good to have some alone time together. "He seems like a nice kid. Why? What do you think about him?"

"He's no Max, but I like him too. The way he was tonight—respectful, but sort of inappropriate, but never too much so—that's how he is all the time. I think it's amazing. And he always seems to know what to say, to make you laugh or to make you feel good about yourself."

"So, you like him?" The answer had been a little too long to be completely innocent. May couldn't say she disapproved either. Based on tonight, he was a good kid. Not good enough for Ryan, but better than any of the boys she'd brought home for sure.

"Yeah."

May smiled. She should have picked up on that before, but she'd been preoccupied with Chris. There was time now, though.

"Not like that!" Ryan said, a little too quickly for *that* to have never crossed her mind.

"Well, if there ever is a *like that*, you'd tell me, right?"

"If anyone shows an interest, you'll be the first to know."

"I'm sure there are plenty interested."

"Yeah, well, I'll believe it when I see it."

"First of all, I know there are people interested. I've scared off at least a few of them, and second—"

"You what?"

May raised a hand defensively. "Oh, only Caleb. You remember him? And what happened to his girlfriend?"

"Oh . . ." Any anger left Ryan's face immediately.

"Trust me honey, I will never scare off anyone who is even remotely good enough for you. You won't need to worry about me scaring off Anthony if you do have a *like that* with him."

Ryan laughed. "Thanks, Mom, but I'm not sure I'm his type. Too young," she added quickly.

Oh, right, May thought.

The boy was Chris's age. While a senior dating a sophomore was not unheard of, they weren't the best relationships either. "Well, forget I said anything. I won't scare him away, but . . ."

"No need to get the shotgun anytime soon. As I said, I don't like him like that. So, there's nothing to worry about."

The boys clomped down the stairs.

"Hey, Mom?" Chris asked before coming into the kitchen. He stopped in the doorway. "Umm, can we drive Anthony home tonight? Something came up with his dad."

"Nothing bad!" Anthony interjected. "Some work thing or something came up. He just won't be able to pick me up, but nothing's wrong."

"Sure," May said, making a mental note to speak with Chris about how he prefaced some requests.

"Thank you."

"Don't mention it."

May yawned as the song faded completely to silence. "Only thing is we might need to call this party over a little early—late as it is. I'll fall asleep at the wheel if we stay up much longer."

"It's not even eleven," Chris said, but he wasn't complaining. He was just giving her a hard time, like all sons do.

"Yeah, well some of us have work in the morning."

"You work from home," Ryan said. "You can start at two if you want to."

"I said some of us. Not me." But as much as the kids liked to joke about her not having a job, there were those deadlines coming up. It would be a busy day tomorrow.

Anthony laughed. "I should get going as it is. Dad wanted me to head on back home. I think he just didn't want me taking the bus this late, but I shouldn't worry him about me getting home anyway."

"Alright," May stood. "Let's head on out then. You live on Mercer, right?"

Anthony nodded. That wasn't too far away.

"It was nice seeing you again," Ryan said.

"Same."

They hugged briefly.

Then the four of them made their way to the door.

"We should be back in about half an hour," May said.

"Text before and after."

"Ha-ha."

The boy's apartment building was sandwiched in the middle of a long line of dark gray towers. Old air conditioners poked through some of the windows, and lines of clothes hung from others. The first three floors all had metal bars on the windows, and a few concealed broken panes, covered by cardboard squares. Just like her old building growing up. A few streets over and it would be hers. The only noticeable difference was the missing flowers spray-painted along every open space of boarded-up window. May's gaze lingered on the blank walls. When was the last time she'd talked with Tay? Chris couldn't have been more than a few weeks old. Would her fingertips still be stained from all that paint?

"That's my window. Fifth floor," Anthony said, interrupting her train of thought as he pointed.

His window didn't have anything blocking it, but the light was off so there was nothing to see. Chris mumbled something; not sure what. The strip of sidewalk outside was mostly clean. Someone inside probably went out to sweep. Usually, one of the kids was made to do it.

She'd done it herself. She'd do the sweeping as Tay cut out stencils and tossed the scraps in with the trash. Cesar hung out with them sometimes too—when the boys weren't off doing there thing. He'd always try helping, fumbling with the pan as Tay sang old-school rhymes and Method Man songs. Together, they made that small doorstep perfect.

"See you in the morning?" Chris asked.

Anthony climbed out of the car, smiling. "You bet."

May watched as Anthony stepped over the garbage-filled gutter to reach the door like it was nothing. And to him, it probably was. She'd done the same herself. Rude Street was worse. There, no one even cared if the streets were clean or not. Of the few who did, none could find the resources to keep anything clean for longer than a day; they gave up or moved on. She had just stepped over and around the broken glass and trash. She'd keep her eyes down, sometimes searching for a pretty piece to take home, even made a small pile of colored glass in her window. The morning light would shoot across it and splash along her wall, coloring it all sorts of shifting shades.She looked back up toward the boy's window. Did he collect anything like that?

He reached the door and unlocked the metal gate without so much as a glance around him; maybe he looked to his music instead. No need to look around for beauty when you could make it yourself. Could he, though?

"Chris, if Anthony ever needs anything. Tell him he can count on us, okay? Anything. Dinner, a place to stay the night . . ."

"They're not that bad off, Mom. I mean, they aren't rich, but they have food. They aren't starving."

"I know. But things can change so quickly. One missed bill or accident and . . . You don't need to tell him tomorrow, and hopefully you'll never need to offer, but just know. If anything does come up, I will say yes."

She pulled away from the curb, glancing back in the mirror as they re-entered the street. What type of person would she be if she didn't offer help? If others hadn't helped her, she would be long dead, or hooked on pills.

Without Chris.

If Ryan's parents hadn't taken her in, without question or reservation. She never would have gotten out. And if she could help someone else do the same, if she could help Anthony leave Mercer and never look back, God, she would do it. Only a monster would ever force someone to spend a night in that slum, let alone a lifetime.

Chapter 6

All Hell

FATHER GREEN HADN'T CLEANED much in the last few months. School was starting in three days, but it still looked like the poor father had just moved in. The mess of his move-in had been taken over by new projects. Piles of flyers advertised St. Francis's biggest event: a track race. It had only taken the father a few months, but it seemed like the track meet was going to be fun.

May gestured to one of the fliers. "The boys are all signed up."

Father Green raised an eyebrow. "The boys?"

May nodded. Chris, Anthony, and Scott had all signed up for the race. As much as they liked to talk about being excited for Father Green's new sports ministry stuff, Chris probably just wanted to brag about his new-found athleticism. He and Anthony had been training together for the last two months and Chris would want to show off.

"So things are going well?"

"Yes."

There was definitely a lot to talk about. Their last meeting had been almost a month ago, back when she had first let Anthony spend the night.

"There haven't been any problems with Anthony coming over. Chris and Ryan love him and it seems like they're being a good influence too. He's even joining us on the family outing today to Asim's for Brownie Town."

"And Elizabeth?"

"She's starting to come around to the whole idea." May smiled and Father Green leaned back in his chair. Elizabeth and Matt had spent a good week trying to talk her out of letting Anthony spend the night. "I said they were scared he'd steal something, right? Or maybe that he'd be a bad influence? Well, if anything the opposite's true. Chris's happier than he's been in months and he's more open now than ever."

Seemed like they talked for hours a day. They were sharing things from their lives again. Anything and everything. Only thing they didn't talk about much was his gay thoughts. He'd put those behind him.

"I still can't thank you enough," she said. It had been a collective effort, but Father Green and Anthony had helped Chris through that hard time. Her little boy was doing fine now, thank you, God, but there was still more to learn and do. Prevent a backslide from occurring. "I finished those books you lent me."

"And?"

"And I don't know. I still don't think it's right." She paused, but it wasn't as simple as that. Father Green nodded for her to continue. He was always so patient with her: waited for her mouth to catch up with her thoughts. "There's that passage in Matthew about marriage. The one where Jesus says not everyone's called to it—"

The father's phone rang. He glanced toward it, but just tapped mute and flipped it over. "Sorry about that. Please, continue."

May swallowed. That was kind of him. A lot of people would've taken longer to ignore it, or taken it to quickly type out a *can't talk now* text. But he'd just turned it away.

"It says that not everyone is called to be married," May continued. "One of the books you gave extended that idea to homosexuals as well. She wrote that . . ." She paused again. How had the line gone? "*Not all men are meant to be with a woman. Some are meant to be single—to join the priesthood—and some are meant to be with a man.* But I don't know if I believe that. I don't see homosexuals anywhere in the Gospels."

"True, Jesus doesn't speak on the topic of homosexuality as we know it directly, but there are examples of how we—"

The father's phone rang again.

He sighed and muted it.

"Someone must really want to talk," May said. The father could take the call if he needed to. It was polite to decline it, but church business was more than a reasonable excuse to be a little rude.

"I'll get to their message in a few minutes. It's from the Bishop's office, but it's probably not an emergency. As I was saying, there are other places to look outside of the Gospels for guidance. There's the other books in the Bible, and there's church tradition."

"Which says it's wrong, doesn't it? At least, that's what I thought, but the books claimed the issue was new—that tradition wasn't in place for sexuality yet."

"In part, yes. Though I have some disagreements with those texts. Modern sexuality is a new concept, one the church is still finding its footing on. We're the same as the rest of the world in that regard. God is living—the spirit is living. To say we can't continue to interpret God's word is to say God cannot still speak with us. But that doesn't mean there isn't tradition to follow. We may not have the letter of the law yet, but there's still the spirit—"

His phone rang a third time. Father Green reached to mute it again, but May said, "Take it."

He glanced to her as if asking if she were sure.

"It must be important."

"Alright. This will just be a moment." He answered the phone. "Father Green."

May sat back in the chair. What could the call be about for the same person to call three times without a message?

"He is?" Father Green sat up straighter in his chair. "What time?" He looked to his watch. "Alright, I'll be there as soon as I can." He hung up, "I need to go. I'm sorry, May. The Bishop had a meeting scheduled with the Cardinal for tomorrow, but now it got moved to today, and . . ." He sighed.

"It's alright," May said. Lord knew she'd had her fair share of meetings and dates changed on her. This meeting, for one. They'd hardly started and he had to leave.

"Would you mind rescheduling to after Mass next Sunday? Not two days from now, but the week after?" he added.

"That should work for me." May stood, smiling. Couldn't let the father see her annoyed, especially since she was the one who'd told him to answer the call. Next week would work fine, after all. She'd need to ask Elizabeth to take the kids home, but that could be arranged easily.

"I'm so sorry to cut this meeting short."

"Don't worry."

"But I do." He smiled. "In the meantime, I'd suggest you read Romans. Particularly the second half, chapters 9 and onwards. The whole book is wonderful, but those chapters are the most relevant. They speak about the spirit of the law in light of Gentile conversion and they're a good starting place for discussion about that."

"Yes, father."

"And May? Good luck with Brownie Town. I hear that thing's huge."

"You met with Father Green, didn't you?" Elizabeth asked a half hour later as they sat in the garden where, thank God, some of the bonnets had survived! Not all of them, but enough to call the summer a success. "What was that about?"

"Oh, just Anthony spending the night," May lied. There was no reason to talk about Chris's trouble when it was so close to being over. "He thinks it's going well too."

"I'm glad it's worked out. I was just afraid you were taking too much, too fast."

"It's alright." May waved her hand, as if brushing off her friend's apology. It wasn't needed. She had actually talked about it with the father back when Anthony first spent the night, and they'd decided Elizabeth was just being cautious. "You were worried about me. There's nothing wrong with that."

They worked in silence. May pulled at the weeds while Elizabeth poked and prodded the flowers, running her fingers along them, looking for who-knew-what before watering each one. May gathered the weeds into a bag then sat back. Maybe she should bring up the truth of the meeting. Father Green had helped, but he still wouldn't give any answers. Elizabeth might be able to help with that.

"Hey! Ms. Flowers! Mrs. Stracke!" Anthony called, walking toward them and interrupting her own thoughts before she could make a decision.

May looked over at him. The boys were hanging out before the concert. He must have been dropped off by his father, Tracy, at the end of the block. Funny how they'd only ever seen each other through a car window.

"How's the garden?" Anthony asked.

"It's survived."

May smiled as she stood. She'd get to know Tracy when the time was right.

"More like thrived, I'd say. Look at them!"

The front door opened before May could respond and Chris and Ryan walked outside.

"Ready?" Ryan asked, holding up the curse jar. She probably couldn't wait to head out to Mrs. Asim's Ice Cream Shop. The jar wasn't filled yet, they hadn't put in much since the beginning of summer, but Brownie Town was leaving the menu after today, so they were going with what they had. If it wasn't enough, well, they could always make up the difference.

"We were just talking about the flowers."

"Wait?" Chris asked. "Like us or the plants?"

"The garden, sweetie."

"Oh. Yeah, they're doing good." He looked toward Elizabeth. "Right?"

Elizabeth nodded with May. They were certainly doing well.

"Mom?" Ryan repeated her question.

"One moment, one moment," she rolled her eyes to Elizabeth. "Brownie Town isn't going anywhere. Let me wash my hands, then we can go."

She brought the bag of weeds in with her and when she returned outside, the kids stood in a small triangle by the car. Elizabeth had already gone back to her house. Strange to leave without a goodbye, but it was a hot day and they'd spent a good while outside.

"How much is in there?" Anthony asked.

"Twenty-six, forty-eight," Ryan said. She must have counted it while May gardened with Elizabeth.

He whistled, but stopped short. "Wait, that's actually not that much. Haven't you guys been filling this for a while?"

"Since February."

"Oh. Well, that's not much cursing then. I thought you guys must cuss all the time with you needing a jar."

"It's mainly for loose change now." May shot the boy a look and climbed into the car. They didn't need the jar. Not really.

"That makes sense. I figured you must just be on your best behavior whenever I'm around."

"We do that too," Chris said. "We plan our cursing around your visits."

Ha! May shook her head. If they planned cursing around anyone, it was her.

"Speaking of plans," Ryan said. "How are we going to do this? Just go at it, or what?"

"I say we just each take a corner and go at it," Anthony said.

"Sure, but I think we should be smart about it too. Like, we start with the ice cream and save the brownies for last. That way we won't have to drink the melted stuff."

"I was going to say the opposite," Chris said. "Brownies first. Drinking the ice cream will be easy."

May parked the car and tried looking in through the ice cream shop's windows. Everything looked the same on the outside, but Mrs. Asim had done extensive remodeling. Scott had told her it was now like a fifties-themed ice cream parlor, and he wasn't lying. The walls and booths had been given a new coat of paint; they were now a bright red and white and Frankie Valli played over the PA.

She shook her head. It seemed like a move in the wrong direction. The old modern look of her shop was nice, but Mrs. Asim seemed to know what she was doing. Scott had said most people liked the changes.

"Hey guys!" Scott called from behind the counter. "You here for Brownie Town?"

"Yes, sir."

"Alright, that'll be thirty-two, forty-six."

"Thirty-two dollars?"

"It's twenty-nine, ninety-nine before tax, and it's actually a pretty good deal for how much you get."

May's eyes got wide. Unbelievable. They should have invited Elizabeth along, and Matt too if it really was that big.

Scott held up the jar and seemed to weigh it in his hands. "How much do you guys have?"

"Twenty-six, forty-eight."

"Oh! Twenty-six, seventy-three." Anthony bent over to pick up a coin. "Damn. Just a nickel, but hey, twenty-six fifty-three."

Anthony put the coin in the jar. Ryan coughed and gestured at the jar on the counter. "Twenty-seven, fifty-three actually."

"What?" he looked confused from Ryan to the jar, then back. "Oh! Oh, sorry." He fished a dollar out of his pocket and put it into the jar. "Sorry."

That was certainly one way to make up the difference.

"Hell, Anthony." May said, smiling. Cursing wasn't right most of the time, but fine every once and awhile—as long as they didn't take it too far. "No need to apologize. We still need four dollars."

"Shit!" Ryan said. Three more.

"You ass, I wanted to say that."

"Like Hell you did."

"Dammit guys, stop arguing! We only have one left."

"Aww, shoot. We can't curse anymore," May snapped her fingers in a short outburst. That had been . . . interesting. At least no one had said one of the real bad ones. Besides, the kids seemed to like it. Ryan and Anthony were all smiles; Chris smiled too, but he was looking around as if he was nervous about Brownie Town. Maybe he was just eager to get started.

"You . . ." Scott shook his head, at a loss for words. "You guys just made my day. Thanks for that. I'll get one Brownie Town right on out to you."

"Well, that was fun," May said as they took a booth close to the counter. They left the jar on the counter for Scott to count.

"Are all your trips like this?" Anthony asked.

"Pretty much."

"There's less cursing, usually," Ryan said.

"Sometimes more," Chris added.

"Yeah! Like the time we went to the aquarium."

"That was a good time."

"Too bad we can't go back," May said. They had no idea how much trouble that had gotten her in. Not to mention, Elizabeth still brought *the aquarium* story up at least twice a year.

"What happened?" Anthony asked.

Scott came back to the counter holding a giant bowl—one of those you would use for popcorn at home—overflowing with ice cream, whole brownies, syrup, whip cream, and at least a dozen cherries.

Chris looked like somebody'd hit him. Maybe he really was anxious about Brownie Town. No reason for him to be. It wasn't like anyone would force them to finish if they couldn't—when they couldn't.

"Hey, Scott?" Ryan asked. "Remember the aquarium?"

He set Brownie Town on the table with a surprisingly loud thunk. May lifted her spoon. It looked tiny beside Brownie Town. They really should have invited more people to join them for this. Chris glanced between Anthony and Scott.

May knew what was going on then: Chris was worried about hanging out with Anthony as Scott worked. It might not seem fair to him. There wasn't anyone else in the store. They might be able to invite the boy to join them. He could sit and talk at the very least until somebody came in.

"Yeah, there's no way you can go back there."

"What did you guys do?" Anthony asked.

"I didn't do anything," Scott said. "It was these two who got the place shut down for a day."

"It wasn't shut down for a day," May corrected. "Only an hour or so. And just the one hall. Honestly, Scott, you're just like your mother. Every time she tells this story, the octopus gets bigger or the—"

"—octopus?"

"She attacked me with it," Chris said, glaring at Ryan. Even after all these years, and even though he loved to laugh at the story too, it seemed like he couldn't ever let go of that glare.

"I did not!"

May sighed. She had mediated this argument more than enough times. "Chris, she did not attack you with it, but Ryan, you did make it squirt ink on him."

Scott giggled. "You should've seen it. She was running around like it was a gun or something."

May looked over at Chris. He quietly dug into his brownie, not looking down and put out but not engaging in the conversation much either. But he was a teenager and his mood would change by the time this story ended. If it didn't, well, they could always talk about it later.

"I still think we shouldn't have gotten banned," Ryan said.

"We probably weren't until you got the head of security covered in ink too, but you just had to *fight the man* didn't you?"

"He was mean."

May couldn't say anything against that. In Ryan's defense, the head of security was incredibly rude.

"How?"

"He thought Mom was kidnapping me."

"What? No, nevermind. But like . . . how in the he— how did you get an octopus?"

"I picked it up," Ryan shrugged.

Her little girl had never explained how exactly she got ahold of that octopus. At the time, she'd just said it came to her and she was trying to put it back when Chris came over, and she'd stuck with that story.

Chris raised his spoon as if he were about to disagree, or finally add something to the conversation, but then just shrugged and went back to eating his quarter.

"But in any case," Ryan said. "That trip had the most cursing."

"Most of it by Mom."

"Really?"

May sighed, leaning away from Brownie Town. Anthony stared at her with his mouth slightly open, like he was impressed. He probably liked this new fact about her: she could curse after all. There wasn't any sense in trying to hide that information.

"Yes, but I made up for it with the swear jar. I put five dollars in—"

"—should've been like fifty."

"—and we decorated it the next day," May finished, ignoring Ryan's comment, though if she was being honest she should have put in a whole lot more money. Everyone got an earful that day. Ryan, Chris, the security guard who had her children cuffed together, and herself. She'd spent the ride back muttering curses at the mirror for letting them get away from her like that.

"Speaking of which," Scott said. "I should probably get back and count it."

Chapter 7

Lullaby

"Any idea what happened last night?" Matt asked.

May stood with the Strackes in a tight triangle right outside the church doors. Chris and Scott had gotten into a fight last night and the kids weren't telling them anything.

She shook her head. "All he'll tell us is that Chris and him had a falling out."

"Matt thinks we should just give them time to work it out," Elizabeth said.

"School's starting tomorrow," May said. "I bet whatever came between them will be forgotten in home room."

They agreed to wait and see if the boys patched things up on their own, but May started to get worried when the first week of school came and went without any sign of the boys putting whatever it was behind them.

May decided to give them another week before stepping in. If they didn't make nice on their own before the St. Francis track event next week, she and Elizabeth would have to get the ball rolling. The best way to do that would be to remind them of what made them friends in the first place. If that failed, she could just sit the two of them down and tell them to shake and forget about it. It'd be just like they were in middle school again, but things would get better.

At the end of the first school week, Anthony came over to spend the night. After talking downstairs, the boys went up to play that video game of theirs. In the last month, Anthony had gotten as good as Chris and could now beat him about half the time. From their occasional shouts and cries, it sounded like Anthony was winning this time, but no way of being sure.

They didn't come downstairs for dinner until Stacy was there to pick up Ryan. The two girls were going to see a movie before hanging out at Stacy's house for a while, so the three kids wouldn't be hanging out at all.

"Text before and after," May said.

"I know, I know," Ryan said as she rushed out the door.

"She forgot the keys," Chris said.

Anthony picked them up from the bannister where she'd apparently left them and jangled them for emphasis. Sure enough, the door swung open.

"Keys?" Ryan scanned the room as she stepped through the door. Her eyes landed on Anthony, still bouncing them around, the same sort of smile on his face that Chris got whenever he was messing with Ryan.

Honestly, the two of them might as well be brothers. The boys had become incredibly close over the last few months and were now basically inseparable. Maybe that was what caused the fallout between Chris and Scott. He might have gotten a little jealous of Chris and Anthony's relationship and thought he was being replaced.

"Keys!" Anthony called, tossing them in a low arc into her outstretched hand. It all seemed so rehearsed, but it wasn't. Couldn't be.

"Thanks!"

May went to close and lock the door behind Ryan. She and the boys were about to eat homemade buffalo chicken salad. All they had to do was take the chicken out of the slow cooker, set the table, and cut Chris's delicious bread. It wouldn't take long, especially with Anthony pitching in. They'd be sitting down at the table in a minute or two; three if they talked while working.

"Who's winning so far?" May asked.

"It's a tie," the boys grumbled. Apparently, their games went by so quickly that the boys had to keep a running tally for the evening.

Despite their attempted growls, the boys were already back to smiling. May looked back and forth between them. Maybe there was some truth to the idea of Scott's jealousy. He wasn't playing with them after all.

❖ ❖ ❖

May's phone rang at nine-thirty that night. Ryan. What could she be calling about?

"Hey, Mom, I umm . . . I need you to come get me."

"What's wrong?" Without realizing how, she was on her feet: the world rushed and blurred sideways.

What happened?

She grabbed her keys before Ryan could respond. The metal shards fumbled in cold palms. Had to get her.

"Nothing! Nothing, it's just. I . . ."

Gunk caught in May's throat; she forced it back in a hard swallow. Was her girl in trouble? Get arrested for something? No, she couldn't have. She was just at the movies.

"I lied to you. I went to a party after the movie with Stacy. I'm sorry, I'm sorry, I'm sorry—"

"Ryan, it's okay. Just, where are you?"

Oh, God. She could actually be in trouble. Please, God, just let it be something minor. Just a noise complaint: no drug or alcohol charges. Ryan wouldn't touch that stuff, but the cops might charge her anyway.

"I'm at the Shell."

The gas station? So she hadn't been arrested. What was she doing there? It was close to that boy Caleb's house. "I'm sorry, I shouldn't have."

"It's alright." Thank God she wasn't far. They hadn't gone out to a country cabin or something dumb like that. Just a little under a half hour away. She climbed into the car—hadn't told the boys she was leaving—but they'd be fine. It'd only be for an hour.

"Caleb brought out this baggie," Ryan said. "And I just—I'm sorry, Mom. I'm sorry."

"It's okay, I'm not mad." May kept her voice steady. She couldn't let Ryan hear any panic. Everything would be alright. "Are you at the Shell by his house?"

"Yeah," Ryan sighed. Her voice trailed off a little. Enough that she was probably already kicking herself for everything.

"You did well, Ryan. I am so, so proud of you."

As May pulled in, the car lights rolled across the gas station, shining against Ryan, who jerked up and lifted her hand in a slight wave. Thank God she was safe.

Ryan met her at the front door. The gas station's cool air flooded out as the doors swished open. Ryan slipped through them to collapse heavily into her arms.

"Are you okay?"

A dreadful weight overwhelmed her. What had happened at the party? Had Caleb done something else? Something Ryan wasn't telling her?

"I'm fine." Ryan nodded against her shoulder. "I just want to get home."

"Did anything happen?"

"No."

"Ryan, you can tell me. If anything—"

"No! Mom, nothing happened. I just . . . I've been sitting here long enough. I think I'm loitering by this point." Ryan tried forcing a smile.

"Alright." The weight lifted, if only a little. Ryan seemed okay, but she could just as easily be putting on a brave face.

"I'm fine, Mom. Really."

Ryan pulled away and trudged to the car. Ryan folded both arms over her chest, as if wrapping herself into a hug even as May pulled her close. She kept one arm around her sweet girl and half-guided them from the gas station.

"I think I'm just embarrassed," Ryan mumbled. She didn't try to pull away though. "I mean, I practically ran from the party. Who does that?"

"People who don't want to get caught up in that shit."

Ryan gasped, but smiled—a real one, this time, too. "Mom! That's a dollar."

And that's all it took for the weight to lift.

"Let's see what the boys are doing," May said, climbing out of the car. Ryan held her phone tightly. Stacy must not have responded to any of the texts yet.

"No!" Ryan almost yelped. "I can do that."

May gave her a quizzical look. She could certainly come too, if she wanted, but it was time to say good night to the boys then head to bed. "Nonsense. I need to check on them before I go to bed, and no offense honey, but I can't see how you function this late."

"But—"

"I'm not saying you can't come too, if you kids want to stay up all night, be my guest. It is the weekend after all."

"Oh, umm . . . okay," Ryan mumbled as she pulled out her phone. May shook her head. Her little girl was certainly behaving strangely tonight. Must have been leftover nerves. "Wait! Good night, Mom. I . . . I love you."

"Love you too, honey." May climbed up the stairs. "I'll see you in the morning."

May paused at the stop of the stairs. The light from Chris's room was on. If the boys were awake, they were sure being quiet.

"Shit!" A voice said. What? Was that Chris?

A scuffle through the door.

Thud!

May placed a hand on the doorknob and cocked her head to the side. What in the world?

"Chris?" May opened the door. "Is everything . . .?"

A leg thrashed: tangled in covers. Dark fabric knotted and twisted against light skin. A choking, almost strangled cry: "God!"

The leg twisted free, turned over, rolling to hide, bury itself into the carpet. Bare bottom stuck in the air.

What . . . when . . . didn't . . . Chris . . . when . . .

May tore her eyes from the bed. A boy stood beside it. Pale skin. Legs reddened from hurried jerking at the pants stuck on his heel.

"Sorrysorrysorrysorrysorry . . ." The mumbled chant swiftly rose in pitch.

Made it hard to think. *Why . . . him . . .* That word above the rest. *Him.* The boy she'd let into her home.

". . .Sorrysorrysorrysorrysorry . . ."

The boy was hunched over. Red-faced. Hair covering his eyes. His mouth didn't stop moving, not even for a breath. Words kept pouring out.

". . .Sorrysorrysorry . . ."

Him. She'd helped *him* apply to college. Just last week. Helped *him* outline an essay. *Describe a trial in your life and how you overcame it.* His mother dying. Oh, poor child. Now, *him* and her sweetie. In her house!

She turned away. Blue paint separated the door from white walls. They'd painted it as a family. Her, Ryan, and Chris. No one else. Their family had been together then. Painting. Alone. Together.

"Get out." Her voice came out as a whisper.

The boy stopped mumbling.

She could hear a soft tambourine. "Lullaby" filled her head. They'd listened to The Cat Empire the whole time they'd painted. The kids had just gotten into them: dancing around to the bright brass. Hardly a moment of quiet since.

"Mom?"

The dam burst inside her. "Get out!"

PART TWO

No Longer There

Chapter 8

The Lost Song

THAT BOY RUSHED OUT of the room, clothes bundled in arm. May slammed the door closed behind him and didn't take her eyes of Chris the whole time. Bedsheets wrapped around his waist; the evidence of their indiscretion hung thick in the air between them. She scrunched her nose at the affronting stench. Made her head fuzzy. Questions wouldn't form. Or thoughts even. Only a pulsing heartbeat in her head.

Chris breathed heavily, skin gleaming with sweat, eye fixed, frozen and half-glazed toward the wall. May's stomach clenched. Why wasn't he looking at her? He couldn't even look at her.

He stood beside the bed: back half-hunched, hair messed up in places, matted down in others. His face pale and sweaty. Lips hung open, twitching slightly as if he was trying to form words but couldn't quite force out the air.

He glanced at her. Barely a second passed before his eyes fell back down. His shoulders slumped further. One hand started kneading the sheet against his hip.

"Mom . . ." His lips barely moved. He clenched the sheets, knuckles shaking.

The pulsing in her head stopped, just for a moment, and froze in her head mid-beat. A pounding rush roared in, like suddenly rolling down your windows on the interstate. The clamor closed in around her. His room was too small. There wasn't enough space. Enough time. It was too late. Too soon. She couldn't—not now. Not here.

"Not now." Her ears rang with the words; a bright, piercing yowl for her to get out. "In the morning."

Chris didn't move. Didn't look up. Didn't do anything to show he'd heard her.

But she had to leave. Had to get out of that room. Get away from that stench.

The doorknob was hot in her hand. Fresh air swarmed through the opening door. Breeze from the AC swept along her clammy arms, spreading cold goosebumps from wrist to elbow.

The ringing stopped with the soft click of the closing door. Her head cleared. Cool wood pressed into her. She leaned back, and her head thudded against the wood.

"God, what do you want me to do?" she whispered the prayer, making the sign of the cross. "Just show me the way, and I'll do it. Whatever it is, no matter how hard, I'll do it. Anything to let him be himself again."

She found herself sitting on the ground with her back pressed up against the door. One hand wrapped over the other; fingers traced the Decade's beads around her wrist.

"Hail Mary." The prayer slipped under her breath, just loud enough to hear. One bead at a time. Pausing over each to say the words. "Hail Mary." Small, warm, metal balls glided across her wrist. "Hail Mary." She stopped to ask for help, guidance, anything at all.

May dropped both hands into her lap. Why hadn't Father Green helped? If only he'd just given a straight answer; told her what needed to be done. He'd given her books about love, acceptance, family. Anything and everything that wasn't homosexuality. He'd just stared at her with that gaze, judging her. Eyes cold and distant, telling her she had to explain herself, not understanding what it was like.

That was all they'd ever done. Everyone at St. Peter's treated her like an outsider. She never should've left home, gone in with these people. They'd taken her boy and . . . and helped raise him. May deflated. They'd taken her and her sweetie in and helped—maybe not enough, maybe not with this, but they'd done their best same as her. Maybe he wouldn't have fallen into this sin back on Rude Street, but he might have fallen into others. Probably would have. Her blood was just cursed to sin. She'd had Cesar, he had *that boy*. Only with her sweetie, she wouldn't turn him out. Not like her parents. She could do everything Henry and Stephanie had done: help him get better. If only there was some guidance.

There had to be other mothers whose sons had turned from God's path. They could help her like Father Green hadn't. There was that one woman with a lesbian daughter. She'd tried writing to May's column, but she hadn't responded. Somebody else might have.

Somebody had to have responded. She could find them. Track down answers. Figure out what she could do to turn her little boy back to the right path.

May could find everything she needed online. She turned toward the stairs—the computer. She should've looked online for another mother's opinion before trusting the father. He was a priest, after all, not a real parent.

Ryan was sitting on the couch, her legs pulled up against her chest. She stared straight ahead.

"Mom?"

"Everything's alright."

Even if it wasn't now, it would be soon. Couldn't let Ryan worry in the meantime; it would be alright in the morning. She would find out what to say, figure out what she needed to do to save Chris. Then, they could leave all this behind them.

"Chris is asleep and . . ." She took a breath, her chest light and faint. "We'll talk in the morning."

"You still love him, right?"

Only her lips moved.

The words pierced her. "What? Of course I do. No matter what happens, I will always love him. And you. There's nothing either of you can do to change that."

Ryan looked up and smiled, but it was one of those tired smiles that doesn't show any teeth and hardly reaches past the lips: more relieved than happy. She must have been sitting there worried ever since they came home.

"Get some sleep, honey."

May helped Ryan to her feet and watched her climb the stairs before turning to face the dark computer. Everything would be alright. If only it could be true this time . . .

Ryan seemed to understand what was going on. She must have found out when Anthony ran downstairs, but had remained calm about it. She would've known her brother was strong enough to escape that boy's bad influence.

May pulled open a browser and started a search. The first article she found wasn't helpful. Not in the way she was looking for at least.

Don't get angry with him. Refocus anger to grief.

She clicked away from the site—there wasn't any anger. He'd done something wrong, vile, and stupid. But she should have done more to stop it: forced Father Green to help, sat down and talked it all out. Made sure her son was doing better. Checked in on him. Not just sat back, trusting him to get better. She should have done more; reminded him about what happened with her and Cesar.

In the end, it was her fault.

The next article echoed this feeling:

Homosexual behavior is often caused by neglectful parenting.

She blinked back tears, her vision a watery blur. She closed her eyes, forcing the tears to roll down her cheeks. So it really was her fault. God, it was her fault. She should have stepped in to stop it. Should've known Chris was vulnerable. For God's sake! Chris said he wished Anthony was gay! She'd let that temptation into the house. Into his bedroom.

It was up to her to fix this. She opened her eyes, dabbed away the tears, and started a new search: how to fix homosexuality.

Can homosexuals change? The first article to pop up was from a Christian forum. A long block of text filled the first section of the page. She scanned through it, skipping through sections about what the Bible said. Great information, but where were the answers?

A bolded line jumped out at her: the path to change.

Homosexuals can change their behavior. As with alcoholism, change is a process. It can't happen overnight and it can't happen without love, support, and dedication.

A link at the bottom of the page mentioned a church site. James Retreat. A camp for gay Christians. Below it dozens of comments screamed at her. All-caps, curse-filled posts calling the retreat a *straight camp*. They talked about abuse, electrodes, and experiments straight out of science fiction. Only a monster would send their kid to something like that. But one comment stood out.

Please, just click on the link. There are some bad places out there, but this isn't one of them. James Retreat helped my son. He can actually talk with me now about all this. It's probably not for everyone, but please. Look into it before listening to all the hate.

She clicked on the link. That commenter was right: James Retreat sounded good. None of the stuff the others had warned about. There was prayer right alongside traditional camping activities. Only difference between it and a summer camp was that it was meant for kids struggling with their sexuality.

The page bragged about all the kids they'd helped. A safe place to talk about proper relationships. Chris could go there. Of course, she'd have to send him away for two weeks. Hard enough letting him spend a night at Scott's, let alone weeks at some camp in Minnesota.

She relaxed her shoulders and breathed. She wouldn't send Chris there. Not unless things got even worse. If Father Green refused to help, give them a straight answer, then, and only then, would she think about sending her boy away.

She bookmarked the page and opened a new tab, another search: *how to talk with your son who thinks he's gay.* That didn't seem right. It didn't get to the spiritual root of the problem. There would be answers, posts written by anyone with an opinion, but there wouldn't be the Holy Spirit in those posts. She added *Christian mother.*

Blog posts and articles filled the results: *Huffington Post, New York Times.* But nothing for mothers by mothers. About halfway down, a dot-org site. Something called *Encourage,* a ministry dedicated to the spiritual needs of parents, siblings, children, and other relatives of people suffering same-sex attractions. And a Catholic ministry too!

The links inside looked promising too:

Homosexuality: just another cross to bear.

Love the Sinner.

Your child is perfect in the eyes of God.

Encourage chastity, don't discourage life.

Living a God-focused life.

Oh, thank you. These were people who knew what she was going through. All of them had sons and daughters—family members who engaged in that temptation. They understood what it was like to see her little boy do something disgusting. They knew her struggle with finding the facts and had formed a group, brought together by the shared pain of having their image of their child's future snatched away. Had made something good: compiled a list of resources and articles, and links to church pages and meeting groups.

All things that could help Chris.

She bookmarked that page as well—no telling if she'd actually be able to find it again in the morning—and minimized the browser.

She pushed herself away from the keyboard, relief seeping through her. There were others like her. She wasn't alone! Thank you, God, for others like her! Parents whose children had struggled with these same feelings and come out the other side healthy, clean, and happy. Others had done it and they could too. In the morning, Chris would go speak with Father Green, make confession for giving into temptation, and after that—a new beginning. Everything would be okay.

It had to.

A high-pitched squeal broke the dark silence. It was late. A soft pale yellow light creeped in from outside: an old streetlamp barely illuminated the outline of May's dresser. The rest of the room was dark, not even a sliver of light from the hallway.

Another squeak. Ryan must be sneaking into Chris's room.

May closed her eyes. She should go join them. It wasn't like she could go to sleep anyway. They could talk about it together, all three of them as a family, but she stayed in bed. She clasped her hands together; fingers interlocking. Better to stay away for now. Ryan could talk to him better without her there. She could be the good little sister and comfort him, help him, just as she had after Lisa had cheated on him.

Maybe in the morning, they would talk about it together; sit around the couch on the living room and make everything better. But for now, for the night, the kids needed to be left alone.

She pulled on a robe and slipped downstairs. Which was more important? Having a good breakfast and waking the kids in the process, or delaying their arrival? She stopped by the kitchen door. She needed more time. There were too many articles to read, too many voices to listen to, and Chris was too important. She'd have to read more, but she also shouldn't skip breakfast—that change would only draw attention to the issue. She'd have to do both.

May read through advice on her phone as the bacon cooked. Her screen smeared with grease, blurring the edge of the page whenever she swiped down.

Letting him find his way.

She skimmed through the featured article about how to talk with your child. The author's son had come out to her two years ago.

You have to let them find their way back to God. I couldn't force my Johnny out of his sin. Trying to make him break up with his boyfriend would just drive him further away. I had to encourage him to make the right choice. But if they choose sin, you can't chase after them. You have to let them go.

May stared down at the bubbling bacon-grease. Could she send Chris away?

She scrolled down. Dozens of comments followed: parents saying how hard it was to watch their child slip into sin, but, in the end, it was the right thing to do. Their children came back. They weren't sinners anymore.

May transferred the bacon to a plate. She couldn't send him away. James Retreat would have been hard enough. There was no way she could let him walk out, but if that was the only way . . .

Before she had an answer, Ryan arrived downstairs. She wore the same clothes as last night, her hair tied back in a haphazard bun.

May turned off the phone. She wasn't ready.

"Good morning, honey."

Ryan sat down at the table. She didn't pull out her own phone, but she didn't look up either. May glanced. What was she supposed to say? Nothing she'd read had mentioned what to tell their siblings.

"Did you sleep alright?"

"You need to talk with him."

"I know, honey. I will," she sighed. Her girl just wanted the best for Chris. Then she added, "Everything will be alright."

If she said it enough, it might be true. Chris would walk downstairs the boy he was years ago, all lanky arms and messy hair. They could eat eggs and bacon, Chris would dip his strips into a small glob of maple syrup and go on about how syrup was the best thing since sliced bread, and they could go on to the park afterward. The three of them would play, May chasing them around the playground like they used to do every Sunday.

When Chris did come downstairs, he wasn't the boy she remembered. He looked tired as he walked past the cooking meat and slid into the seat beside Ryan without a word, his eyes on the ground the whole way.

"Morning, sweetie."

He glowered up at her, eyes red and narrow.

"Morning," he mumbled, though it felt like a curse. May turned off the stove and moved the rest of the bacon onto a plate. She hadn't even started the eggs yet. She winced. It wasn't enough.

Ryan picked up one of the bacon strips and turned it over in her hand, slowly glancing between them. She bit into it as if showing the two of them how to eat. May swallowed, tried to get rid of that lump in her throat. She couldn't eat, pretend as if nothing had changed. Oh, God. Could they really not eat like a family anymore?

May tried to reach across the table to do the same, to accept that they could continue as if last night hadn't happened, but couldn't move her hand.

Ryan finished her piece of bacon. Picked up another.

May faintly smiled at her own plate. This was good. Her girl was going to wait here with them, and make sure everything worked out.

Ryan finished the second piece too, then stood. May tensed, muscles clamping down, freezing her to the chair.

Keep eating!

Ryan wiped her hands on her pants. "Thanks for breakfast."

She was gone before May could scold her for using pants like a napkin.

After a moment, May managed, "She's smarter than we give her credit for."

"Mom?"

"I know," she sighed. She fought back the desire to bury her face in her hands and give up. "This isn't about Ryan, but . . ." She managed to keep her face up. She had to keep looking at Chris. "I'm sorry, Chris. I . . ."

He met her eye. It shouldn't be this hard for her. She should be able to tell him what he needed to hear. If only knowing that made things easier . . .

"I remember what it was like to be your age. Things are different now, better in some ways . . ." Worse in others. "But the challenges we face, the temptations, those are the same. Drugs, lust . . . Those are the same things I struggled with when I was a kid."

"Mom—"

She raised a hand to stop him. "I know. I know. You aren't on—"

"I'm gay!" He almost shouted the words. "Anthony's my boyfriend. I'm sorry you had to find out that way. I'm sorry you saw us together. I didn't want you to . . ." he trailed off. His eyes went back to the table.

May didn't say anything. The boy needed to speak his mind as well.

Chris took a breath. "I didn't want you to find out we're dating. Not yet."

"Would you have ever told me?"

The question seemed essential right then. He had to know it was a sin; otherwise, he wouldn't have hid it from her.

"Yes. No. I . . ." He shook his head. "I don't think I would have."

"Why wouldn't you tell me?"

"You wouldn't understand."

She deflated, sinking back into the chair, the heat of the moment leaving her. Oh, Chris . . . "Of course I do. Just because it's a sin—"

"Love is a sin?"

"Sex—"

"—with a man?"

"Sex with someone who isn't your wife," May raised her voice over his; the heat returning. He had to understand. Being with a boy would only cause him harm.

"I'm gay! I'm never going to have a wife! Can't you understand?"

"I do! I just . . ." May sighed, an exasperated half growl. Why wasn't he listening?

"What?"

She closed her eyes. He wasn't getting it. If only he'd step back for a moment and see.

"I want you to have a good life, Chris. A happy one." And he could have it, if only he'd listen. She'd made mistakes too, but he couldn't see that.

"And I can't be happy with Anthony?"

"No!" He would never be happy living like that. "It's sin. Plain as that. Wrong." How could she show him? Father Green's books had talked about this. There were gifts of the Holy Spirit in sex. Goodness shared between spouses. "Sex is meant for a man and a woman. For marriage. It can be fun outside of it, I know it can, but it isn't right. There's nothing truly good in . . . that . . ."

His glare crumpled: jaw loosened and eyes softened. "Nothing good?"

"No." May shook her head. He looked down and her heart broke and twisted. She reached over to him, trying to hold onto his hand, but he didn't reciprocate the motion. He sat, stone-faced, unmoving, head lowered.

"But that doesn't mean there's nothing good about you. It's not you— it's not the love that's bad. It's . . . it's . . ." How could she even say it? The word felt wrong—like a brick in her mouth. "It's homosexuality that's wrong."

His head only sank lower. May's breath caught in her throat. She withdrew her hand. Why hadn't he talked with her about this before?

"Sweetie, why didn't—"

"—I didn't want you to hate me." He looked up, just a flick of the eyes, but enough to freeze her blood.

"Hate you?" The words clenched in her stomach. "Chris, I could never hate you."

"You couldn't?" he sat up straighter in his chair. His sleeve blocked out most of his new smile as he wiped the back of his hand across his nose.

"No." May reached across the table to grab his arm. He didn't pull back this time. Good.

He had to know that. She hadn't stopped loving him when he first told her about his problem, and she wasn't going to stop loving him now. His teeth reflected her own smile.

"You're my son. The best part of my day. No matter what you do, whatever sin you fall into, I will always love you."

Chris stared through her, his eyes unfocused and glazed over. His hand loosened in hers and he slumped backward. "Father Green—"

"—we'll go back to him." May squeezed his hand. "Make sure he helps this time around. If he can't, well, I found a bunch of websites and articles that can. Go see him today before lunch. And afterwards, we'll make a plan. Together."

"Okay." His voice sounded faint, seemingly overwhelmed by the stress of the last few days. Months. However long it had been since they could be there for one another.

"Sweetie, everything will be alright." She let go of his hand.

"Okay."

Chapter 9

Miserere

MAY SAT ACROSS FROM Ryan: a few bags of chips lay open between their plates. Ryan's was already empty, but May hadn't even picked up her sandwich yet. She held onto her phone instead. Tapping the screen, the phone's light lit up her lap in steady pulses. Off and on. Off and on: a single text on the screen *Getting lunch with fr.*

May looked down at the phone. Her boy had sent it an hour ago. He must have sent it to Ryan too. She hadn't asked where Chris was when they made sandwiches. She'd hardly said anything since coming downstairs.

She sighed, looking away from the phone. Her girl usually talked, joked, said anything and everything to try and brighten the mood. She'd done it when she was little and too young to know what she was doing. Ever since she'd hugged her leg back on the fifth anniversary of Cesar's death. But now? She was quiet.

Maybe her honey blamed herself for her brother's mistake. She'd clearly tried her hardest to be supportive, but she couldn't help him. She must have thought she'd failed him. But that wasn't true; there was nothing they could've done to stop this.

May swallowed and looked down at the unopened message. There was something they could have done. She was his mom for God's sake! She should have done something. She should've been able to keep Chris from getting this bad. She should've seen Anthony for what he was. She should've . . .

Her vision went blurry.

No. She couldn't cry. No tears in front of Ryan.

"Can I go do homework?" Ryan asked, voice soft. The first thing said since sitting down.

May couldn't say anything back. Her throat closed and restricted. She nodded, letting Ryan go.

Her gaze fell back down to the phone. Chris's text shone on the screen. On a normal day, she wouldn't think twice; send back a quick thanks and leave him with Father Green. But after last night? Could she trust him to do what was right? It was time to text him.

May froze, her fingers hovering over the message:

Getting lunch w fr

What if he hadn't gone to lunch with the father?

"Mom?" Ryan poked her head in through the door. "Are you still using the computer? Mom?"

"Oh," May peeled her eyes from the screen and let the phone slink down onto the table. "Oh, no. No, it's all yours."

She must have forgotten to turn it off last night. If Elizabeth ever found out May had left the computer on overnight, she'd never hear the end of it. She was obsessed with saving power. Had been ever since May wrote to that one mother who needed to cut costs. She'd focused on electricity, which Elizabeth loved for the environmental aspects. She'd even been inspired to try and start up a neighborhood compost bin, but that ended when the flies swarmed the block party. May somehow got half the blame for the whole ordeal even though she'd argued against Elizabeth about the benefits of making a giant, organic trash heap in between their houses. The two of them spent the next week admitting their mistake, apologizing to everyone else, and getting everyone to forgive them.

Elizabeth was always the one to get their neighbors to that last step. She managed to get everyone laughing about some part of the disaster or another. Some of the time, it was at the expense of one of the other neighbors, one who wasn't there, but most of the time it was at her own expense.

She'd spent hours upon hours making the best-looking chocolate-lemon pie anyone had ever seen, only to have a horde of fifty flies descend on it the moment she unveiled it to her panicked public.

Thing is though, as much as she cried and cursed the flies, she could laugh about it the next day. She always knew how to find the good hidden in the bad. May turned the phone over in her hand. She'd know what to do, wouldn't she?

Her phone buzzed. Chris:

OMW

May sighed in relief. He was coming home.

Whamp! The front door closed, startling May. She slipped her Decade bracelet back onto her wrist. They just had to get through today, and everything could go back to normal.

"Chris?" she half rose from the couch, both her legs asleep from her curled position.

He entered the room a few seconds later. His shoulders curled into his body. Somehow, he looked smaller than he did in middle school. He held his head low too, far enough down that she'd have to bend to meet his eye. She hadn't had to do that in years.

He shifted his eyes up to her: wide and open as if waiting for her to say something, anything to keep him as her little boy.

"How was lunch?" May asked. Maybe the talk with Father Green would be enough and they could move past this whole thing and never worry about it again.

"Good."

Her legs tensed against the cushion. Couldn't he talk with her?

"It was . . ." His mouth twitched, halfway between a smile and scowl. How could his body language say so much? He sank down into the couch, curling up his own legs so he lay against the armrest, looking at her. "Father Green says I should hear what you want to say."

"He does?"

Chris nodded.

"About the whole . . ."

"Gay thing?" Chris smiled.

"Now, that isn't funny," she chided, but he smiled so he must know it would be okay after all. "One mistake doesn't have to mean anything."

"A mistake?"

"It's okay, Chris. I went through the same—"

He chuckled. "Please don't tell me about how you and dad used to do it."

Oh, good. At least he was trying to find some humor in this.

"Alright," she forced herself to smile. He had to see she was trying just as hard as he was. "Alright. I won't."

"And it's not the same. Not really."

"Maybe not."

"I mean, you never said you hid from your parents."

"No," she laughed. "But for completely different reasons. I wanted them to know what Cesar, Tay, and I were up to. They didn't control me and they had to know it. I was doing wrong, but I wasn't ashamed."

"I'm not ashamed. There's nothing to be ashamed about."

"It's alright, sweetie. It took me a while—"

"Mom. I'm gay."

She shook her head. *Oh, sweetie.* How long had it taken to get out of that addiction? For months—

"Mom! I need you to hear me—"

—after she stopped using, she had still felt that pang to go back. For weeks, she had thought of herself as nothing other than an addict even though she'd been clean. It would take time, but soon Chris would move past it entirely.

"You think—"

"Mom. You're not listening to me. I'm gay. I like guys."

"And I liked pills."

Chris was on his feet, "Jesus! You're unbelievable."

"Sweetie, sit back down."

"Or what?! You'll send me away?"

She reared back. What? "No! Where's this coming from."

"I saw the website."

"What?"

"You were looking them up! A fucking camp, Mom! You'd really send me away?"

The question tore at her chest. Never. How could he ever think she'd send him away? Looking at the James Retreat website—that had only proved to herself that she could never push him away. Her voice caught in her throat as she tried to speak. Did he think she didn't love him?

"Christ . . ."

Before she could find her voice, he stormed out of the room and the door thundered shut.

Chris wasn't home.

The entryway's light was on. The dark wood of the unlocked door loomed tall in the room. The white walls had always seemed to push on it, made it look smaller than it actually was. But now it stretched up as a giant before her.

May sat on the bottom stair, elbows braced on knees, phone in hand. She couldn't look away from that door. Why wasn't he answering? Or calling back? He hadn't even called Ryan!

Maybe he'd gone to the Strackes, but Elizabeth would have called her. There was still a chance. Maybe he'd called Scott. . .

On the fourth ring, Matt answered. "Hello?" he yawned.

"Have you heard from Chris?"

"No." His voice snapped alert; fully awake now. Elizabeth was probably listening in. "Is everything alright?"

"He's supposed to be home," May squinched her eyes closed as she spoke her half-truth. "I was wondering if he's over with you."

"We haven't seen him. I can ask Scott if he's heard anything."

"Anything would help."

She held the silent phone against her head and waited for Matt to come back onto the line. Chris had to have told someone where he was going. She closed her eyes and pictured his face.

Be there. Be there. Come on sweetie, be there.

The line crackled faintly as Matt's voice returned. "Sorry, May. Scott hasn't heard anything either. I'm sure he's fine. Probably with Anthony."

May almost dropped the phone. That was it. He was with *him,* wasn't he? Over at that boy's house. Living in the slums, choosing to go back to the place she'd worked so hard to bring them out of. And for what?

She managed a weak "Thank you."

"We'll text if we hear anything."

May hung up. Dropping the phone, she collapsed her head into her hands. Her fingers rubbed deep lines into her temple.

She prayed; not even waiting to finish the sign of the cross. *God, let him be safe. Even if he's with Anthony, let him be safe. Keep him from . . . doing that, but please, please just let him be safe.*

"Mom." Ryan's voice jarred her. She stood at the top of the stairs; hair pulled back in a messy knot. "I heard from him. He's at Anthony's."

May released her breath. *Thank you.*

But why didn't Chris go to the Strackes's? Sure, the boys were fighting, but he should've known Scott would forgive any argument for a night. Scott would have done anything to keep Chris in a good home. Out of the slums. They loved each other too much to ever let him spend a night out there.

"Mom?"

May refocused on her daughter.

"Are you going to get him?"

She clenched her jaw shut and forced her eyes closed. Why'd Chris choose that slum? She cried, shoulders shaking. It was for him, wasn't it?

Her sweetie was just going to leave her—leave his faith for that boy? Anthony did this. He turned her boy against her, against God, and undid everything. All her work, all the sacrifice of Ryan's parents, Anthony took it all and destroyed it.

May lay in her dark bedroom, squinting up at the bright square of her phone. It was too much. She threw the phone down and closed her eyes. The Encourage forum told her everything would get better. As if she hadn't told herself that enough already.

It would get better.

How? How could things get better from here?

She wiped her eyes, who cared if her tears dripped onto her pillow. Chris was gone. She'd forced him out. Made him go to Anthony's house.

He must think he's so alone.

If only he'd come home. He'd see then. She loved him.

God, just let Chris come home. Please, I'll do anything if you just help him see you again.

Boom. Boom.

There was a pounding on the front door. Chris?

She ran down the stairs and opened the door. A tall figure loomed in the entryway.

"What the hell is wrong with you?" the man shouted. She knew that voice. Tracy: Anthony's father. He pointed out to the street and continued to yell. "Kicking out your own child like that!"

"I—"

"And you couldn't even wait until the morning? Jesus Christ! You have any idea how dangerous it is walking around there?"

"He ran away." May's voice even sounded weak in her head.

"You let him go!"

"He needs to find his way back." The words from Encourage had rushed into her mind before she'd even thought about them. "Chris is lost, and coming after him before he's ready won't help."

Tracy stared at her. His mouth twitched like he was unable to tell whether he wanted it to hang open or grind his teeth into powder.

"He has to—" she continued.

"You don't love him at all, do you?"

"Excuse me?" May snapped. How could he say something like that?

"If you did, you'd be out there looking for him and doing everything possible to bring him back."

"How dare you? You have any idea—"

"Yeah, actually, I do."

"—what it's like to—"

"They came out to me."

"—see your son running around with a hoodlum?"

"Hoodlum?"

May froze. What had he just said? "You knew?"

Tracy nodded. "Figured you knew too, but guess I shouldn't be surprised."

"What's that supposed to mean?"

"You must be one of the thickest people around."

May's grip tightened around the doorframe.

"You know," he continued. "I can't stand ignorant people like you. Walking around like you're better than everyone else just because you found Jesus or some shit."

"How do you think we feel about people like you? Hmm?" God, this jerk was going to get it. "With your self-assured head so far up your ass—"

Tracy's laugh cut her off.

"That's rich. If anyone's got a head up their ass, it's your son."

May narrowed her eyes; about to slam the door on his face, toes, or whatever he might stick in between to keep it open.

"What are you talking about?"

"You haven't seen him limping in the morning?" Leering, his damn eyes practically shone in the porchlight. He must've thought he'd won, that her son would actually be the one to—

Chris wouldn't. Even if he gave into temptation, he wouldn't be the one . . .

"Oh, you thought it was the other way around?" he laughed again. "Lady—"

"Get the hell off my property."

"May—"

"I said, get out!"

May slammed the door and threw the lock. Her fists shook; nails dug into her palms, threatening to draw blood. She needed a drink, a hit, anything. May advanced on the kitchen. Steps like thunder against the wood floor.

"May?" Tracy's shout muffled by the door; a thud and loud crack. He'd kicked the door. "Fuck!"

She yanked the fridge open, her eyes scanning for any small pleasure she could indulge in. Anything to lie to her brain and tell it *See? I've done my little cheat.* The old Father Lee had told her about it years ago: not a complete replacement for drugs, but good enough—a stupid trick to release some dopamine instead of going back to old habits.

Nothing: only a half empty bottle of Gatorade Chris had left after a run with *him*. She tore it from the shelf and slammed the door shut. The cap slipped to the ground and she upended the bottle, draining it before the fridge's cold air could fade from the room.

It didn't help. It never did.

"Fuck," she hissed through clenched teeth. It felt so good to finally say *fuck* again after all these years. "Fuck. Fuck. Fuck. Damn. Shit. Fucking bastard."

Her gaze lingered on the curse jar: *Shit*, Chris's curse wrapped around the edge of the glass.

They'd worked together; all three of them around the kitchen table. May had spent half an hour digging through the cabinets to pull together their art supplies. No telling where those crusted brushes were now. The Cat Empire was playing, Even back then Chris loved them. Ryan enjoyed their rhythms well enough, but she'd never become as big a groupie as him. Chris had told a story about the game of soccer he and Scott played together, Ryan had kept jumping in—she'd watched the whole thing from beneath the shade of some trees with her friends—and all three of them were laughing. May had shook so hard she had to stop painting and wipe at her eyes. She'd smeared a green streak across her face, which only got Chris and Ryan to laugh harder. May had booped Chris on the nose, leaving behind a nice green glop which Chris had stared at with wide, crossed eyes. Ryan had fallen out of her chair, her sides heaving and gasping for breath in between deep, bright snickers.

Was that all they had left?

May turned the jar over in her hands, the raised paint ticking her fingers. Red and green swirls twisted around and around, stopping at their names: Chris, Ryan, May. The words stood stacked one on top of the other. Ryan's scrunched cursive looped down in between *Chris*. Her long *Y* slipped around the dot in his *I*.

The paint chipped beneath her fingers. *Chris* peeled from the jar; the yellow letters crumbled and drifted to the ground. Jar trembling in hands, the kitchen blurred through shiny tears. The glass slipped and cracked against the table. May shot her hand out to stop its fall; a shard of glass cut along her finger.

"Fuck!" May swept the remains of the jar from the table.

The glass shattered. Fragments rattled across the ground and stopped at Ryan's feet. She stood in the kitchen doorway; hands at her sides, half curled up toward one another, fingers frozen above her knuckles. They didn't shake at all, but just hung there. Unmoving.

"Mom?"

The word seemed to echo somehow.

She took a sliding step forward, moving the glass out of the way with the sole of her socks.

"Stop . . ." May choked on her shout. Ryan ignored her, moved forward, and wrapped warm arms around her. May shook against her girl's shoulders. Blood dripped from her cut onto Ryan's back, who shifted and shivered in the cold kitchen.

"It's going to be alright," she whispered between May's sobs. "It's . . ."

The word caught in her tired throat. Her mouth moved, jaw working up and down in short, uncontrolled quivers. What was there to say? That same lie she'd been saying for months? It wasn't going to be alright. He'd left. He was gone and it was her fault. She did this. Her fault. Her fault. Her fault.

How could it get any better?

She'd failed as a mother.

Oh, God, Chris!

Chapter 10

So Long

IN THE MORNING, THEY drove to Mass.

Ryan took the backseat.

Still nothing from Chris.

Father Green kept the service concise; as though he knew something was wrong. The sermon was shorter and more to the point than usual: be responsible for God's creation. The songs slipped around May, filled the air, and caused her shoes to vibrate with the deep, resonant bass of the church. She used to love closing her eyes and singing along with them—feeling the breath of her church family in her very bones. Today, Chris's voice was absent. The final song left her empty, like she was exhausted and couldn't move. Ryan stayed beside her, looking up at her as if waiting for something, for someone to notice them staying behind.

May looked away from her girl, over toward the altar. She'd sat at the front row when Chris was baptized. Everyone else was behind them, but she imagined it was just her, Chris, Henry and Stephanie, and Father Lee there. The music that day was quiet. A whole lot of slow, low hymns that Stephanie would always swear was done just for her and the sleeping Chris. They'd been coming here as a family every Sunday since then. No matter what happened, they always made it as a family in the morning.

Ryan touched her shoulder. She smiled at May as if to say *It's okay; Chris will be here next week.*

How could she be so sure?

"Meet outside?" Ryan asked.

May nodded, and swallowed hard. What if he didn't come back? Lord knew it had happened before. It'd happened to herself too. She'd fallen into bad habits: first stealing paint with Tay, then sex, then drugs, and one by one, every other vice in the world. She was at rock bottom when Cesar and she became pregnant. Henry and Stephanie had brought her out of it, but without them . . .

The pew creaked, the wood adjusting to Father Green's weight. He sat near her, but not too close. Facing the crucifix, he folded his hands between his knees.

"I'm always intimidated by sermons—by him, really," he began.

May turned to Father Green. He looked sad, maybe tired with small bags under his eyes. Had he talked with Chris last night?

The father gestured up at the cross. "I thought it would get better when I got the collar, but . . . if anything it's worse. I'll sit here before writing the homily and wonder if I could do what he did—or what Peter or Thecla did. I know I should. I'm supposed to be selfless and brave, but that doesn't mean I am. Or that when I have the courage to act that I'll do the right thing."

She turned away from him. It would be rude to show her how disappointed she was. Was this his way of apologizing? He should have been able to help Chris. There'd been enough time to stop things from all falling apart.

"Every time someone comes to me, I'm terrified. Will I say the wrong thing? What if I can't help them? Or, worst of all, what if I lead them the wrong way?"

He turned to face her. "But . . . I can't hide. I'm a priest. That insecurity, that valley of death—that's where God wants me. I have to try, otherwise, if I don't, I know I'll have failed."

"What if they don't listen?"

Father turned back to the crucifix. "You make sure you're there for when they do."

She glanced up; Jesus stared down at her, his wooden face reflecting her pain. Could she do what he did? That was the root of it, wasn't it? She couldn't sacrifice everything she was for someone else; although, she was supposed to. But how could she sacrifice her little boy?

What would that sacrifice look like? Was she meant to give up her own happiness—let her sweet boy run away and let him eventually find his way back—or, bring him home? Go and let him keep thinking he was gay? He'd never change, but he'd be beside her.

That second option seemed wrong. Sin was never the right answer, but forgiveness was. That's what He taught. Even up there, He asked for forgiveness.

"May." She blinked, tearing her gaze from the cross. Father Green reached out to her, hand hovering near her arm. "My sister's coming down for the week. The two of you should meet. Her son came out a few years ago, and it's—it was hard on her, but Alicia, she loves Ralph. She doesn't agree with a lot of what he says, but she loves him."

May glanced over to the father; his expression was unreadable. What did that mean? Maybe this was his way of admitting he couldn't help Chris. Or maybe his way of saying she needed a friend to talk to. Without Elizabeth, who did she really have? She'd left everyone behind when Chris was born. The last thing she'd ever said to Tay was that she'd call her soon, but that was—oh Lord—eighteen years ago.

"Thank you Father, but—"

"May, meet her for coffee. I'll send you the information. Okay?"

She nodded, startled by the bluntness. He couldn't help, that had to be it, but maybe his sister could.

"Good." He stood. "Have a blessed day."

She turned back to the crucifix. Everything was quiet and still; the only noise was the rhythmic click of the father's boots on the hard tile. May rose only after the footsteps had stopped and the door had closed behind the father. She genuflected, bowing to the cross, and retreated out of the church—away from those outstretched arms offering only two choices: sin or failure. Let Chris's soul waste away or disown him.

No. No, it wasn't too late for Chris. It wasn't. She could go and bring him back, change his mind. Do the thing the blogs told her was wrong. She would chase after him—what she should have done the moment the door closed.

But for that to work, he had to return her calls.

Sunlight reflected off the brass handrail; May lowered her gaze to the concrete, and moved onto the church steps and into the bright morning light. Two women sat off to one side: Ryan and Elizabeth. Her friend looked out of place, legs curled at the ankles two steps below, alongside Ryan, who lounged down four steps, her own modesty protected by jeans and a long, yellow blouse. But when she looked past their body language, to their faces, their roles seemed switched: Ryan was uncertain of her place beside Elizabeth. Those sweet blue eyes which normally looked up to greet anyone and everything stared at a fallen leaf she'd crumpled in her hand.

"I'll work on it," Elizabeth promised.

May let the door close behind her. What could that be about?

Ryan nodded, catching sight of May as she did. "Hey, Mom."

"Matt and Scott went on without me," Elizabeth said. "Can I tag along with you?"

"Sure thing," May said, walking towards them.

With a roll of her eyes, Ryan helped Elizabeth back to her feet.

"I'm not that old yet," she grumbled, but took Ryan's hand anyway to pull herself up from the stairs.

May shook her head: almost felt like old times. They walked over to the car without a word. The silence between them was large and heavy like some sort of creature. No one said anything because there wasn't anything to say, nothing to be done. Chris had left, and there was nothing any of them could say in that moment to change it.

Once in the car, Elizabeth cleared her throat as if trying to ease the silence away with a cough. It didn't help.

"How was the first week of school?" she asked, making a second attempt by falling back to the kind of small talk you'd make with strangers.

"Good." Ryan leaned against the passenger side door and sighed. "I'm taking French."

"Is Ms. B still teaching that?"

May's hands went slack on the wheel. How could they make small talk like nothing had changed? Why weren't they asking about Chris, telling her if they'd heard something, promising her they would let her know the instant he approached either of them.

For the next four blocks, they kept talking. The questions thundered in her head as they chatted, not once mentioning her sweet boy. They couldn't have forgotten him so easily. Without her contributing, the small talk slowly trailed off. Silence filled the car again, preventing any of them from doing anything but think about Chris.

May glanced around the road. It was silly, but maybe she could see Chris walking along the sidewalk, or leaving one of the stores. A couple stood outside an old record shop, leaning against the wall like they had all the time in the world. A woman waited to cross the intersection. What would she do if he did appear?

She shook her head. *Go to him.* That's what she'd do: slam on the brakes and run over to wherever he was. Of course for that to happen he'd have to be somewhere near the road.

They passed the old Pizza Hut, now a Chinese place. Chris had first learned to drive here. That all seemed so long ago. Elizabeth had thought May was crazy for letting Chris loose on the road, but he'd been ready. They'd spent the last week going over driving procedure; but on the first day he drove, May had given him the keys after church and had told him to go at it. Ryan had braced her arms between the door and the passenger seat, and had even tried to belt herself in with two seatbelts. But despite Ryan's terror, they had made it home safe in one piece with no incidents at all. Chris had beamed from ear to ear as he jumped out of the car to share his victory over the road with Scott. The only mistake he had made the entire time was forgetting to turn off the car before throwing the door open.

He'd made it home with better control of the brakes than May had ever showed him. Giving him absolute trust had clearly inspired him to drive carefully. He seemed to know what to do from watching her and others drive for fifteen years. All he needed was for someone to give him the keys and say, "Go at it." She'd put him in a sink-or-swim situation, and he'd swam.

But what would she have done if he had sunk? Stop him in the parking lot before it got out of hand? She couldn't have done that, could she? She'd set him up to sink or swim. She'd trusted him to swim, to follow the rules and make it home safely, but, if she stopped him early, what would happen to that trust? It would be gone.

Sometimes you had to let someone go off the right path to bring them back to it. You had to let them make their own mistakes and be there for them when they made their way back. Father Green was right about that. She'd have to be there for Chris when he came back.

May watched Elizabeth inspect the flowers: bending down to turn a plant, tracing her fingers along the stalk, feeling for something, maybe just giving her hands something to do while she looked. Elizabeth stood and shuffled half a step over to the next one before lowering herself to repeat the same inspection.

She cupped one bluebonnet in her hand, its stalk curled down, its flora pulling the plant. May tried leaning forward to get a better look. What was she doing that she hadn't been? Elizabeth shifted, blocking her sight before making a soft *tsk* noise, standing, and moving on to the next. She didn't crouch back down. Instead, she abruptly turned to face May.

"I'm here if you need anything. Or if Chris needs anything, I'm here. Even if you don't, please don't shut me out. I want to help."

"Elizabeth . . ."

What could May tell her? Chris is going to Hell? Thinks he's homosexual?

"You don't need to say. Ryan told me."

"What would *you* do?"

"May, I . . ." Elizabeth took a breath and May thought her whole face looked drained, as if she'd been the one up all night. "I don't know. I can't possibly imagine what you're going through, what Chris is going through. All I can say is he has a place with us. If you can't—"

"What's that supposed to mean?"

"Nothing! Just that if you can't convince him to change back, it would be better for him to be with friends than on the street."

"Don't you think I know that? If he'd been with you, he would've come back in the morning, but he didn't. He ran all the way into the city to be with that boy and he isn't coming back. He's . . ."

She couldn't say that last word or it might come true. Saying it might jinx the whole thing. She almost laughed—the whole thought was stupid; censoring herself as if it could change the fact that her sweetie had run away. Just the same, if anything, any stupid thing, would get him back, she'd do it.

"How could you think I wouldn't give anything to have him back home?"

"I didn't mean it like that."

"Oh?"

"May, you know I think you're a great mom, it's just . . ." She lifted both hands, gesturing vaguely in the air as if that explained anything.

"Just what?"

"We have different values. That's all. You did everything you could to keep Chris from drugs and he's never once touched anything. If you caught him even thinking about smoking weed, I bet you'd have grounded him for so long his skin would be nothing but wrinkles by the time you let him go. But if I came home to Scott with a joint, I'd just yell at him for being a fool and talk to him about not doing drugs."

"So you think you're parenting's better than mine?"

"We have different values, that's all. If Scott tried homosexuality, I'd have smacked him straight on down to confession."

"You do, don't you?"

"Well . . ." Elizabeth reached down to pluck out a dead flower. She straightened and twisted the browned stem in her hand. "You weren't as solid with your theology as you could have been."

"My theology?" Where was this coming from?

"May, Chris is a sodomite. Clearly you—"

"No! You don't get to say that to me. You have no idea what it's like to—to raise your kids alone. To be the good parent and the bad one at the same time. You . . ." her hands shook in fists. The cut on her hand reopened and a small drop of blood rolled down her knuckle.

How could Elizabeth say that to her? She was supposed to be a friend, to comfort her, to lie and say it wasn't her fault, or that it was unavoidable. May turned. The garden seemed to blur and twist, slanting and sliding beneath her. She took a breath. Her oldest friend said nothing, so May left.

By the time she reached the door, she was crying. How long had Elizabeth thought she was a better mother? Had she spent the last decade judging her, sitting back and thinking how much better her kids were doing than her own? Had she known? She had, hadn't she? Elizabeth had to have known Chris was falling into sin. She must have seen it: another lost, fatherless boy.

They never should've left Rude Street. At least there, the people cared for each other. Not like here. That woman knew—she knew Anthony! She knew what he was, but said nothing when May invited him over. She had known and done nothing. It was almost like she wanted him to corrupt Chris. And for what? To prove to all their friends that she was the better mother? That May couldn't do it alone? That she was a failure?

The bitch.

"Mom?" Ryan called from the living room.

"I'll be there in a second," May said, wiping her eyes clean and counting through her breaths. How could one word change so much? Of course they were better off here. Sure, Tay was a better friend than that horrible woman next door, but Ryan was here. Her family was here, should be here.

She held her eyes closed for a moment, then entered the room.

Ryan was sitting with her legs curled against her chest on the far side of the couch. A paper bag lay on her knees and a long strip of painters tape curled up from the brown paper. *May* was written across one side; tape cutting through the edge of the *Y*.

"Yeah, honey?"

"Tracy, he . . . he left a note." Ryan held out the bag.

When you're ready to be a mother again

Chris is at my place.

Tracy

May crumpled the note in her hands. The paper folds bit into her hand. How could he say that? She was a good mother, now and always. Who was he to say otherwise! How many times had she taken Anthony in? Let him stay when he had nowhere to go.

"Mom? Are you alright?"

Ryan sat up. She must have seen the blood on her hand.

May forced herself to breathe. "I'm alright. I just need . . ."

What did she need?

Chris.

"What are we going to do?"

Chapter 11

Feeling's Gone

You can't support their choice. As much as it hurts, you have to keep them away.

May closed out of the tab. They all said the same thing: having a gay son sucks. Some of the posts were kind about it: some parents told about how they were tempted to just look away from their child's sin. Maybe it would go away if they ignored it, but it almost never did. Others hated their children for what they'd done. Those parents took all the shame they felt for having failed their kid and turned it against their sons and daughters, forcing them further away. She couldn't do that to her boy.

She wanted Chris home; not in the slums. But she couldn't go get him. Not yet—not if she wanted him fully back with her. He wouldn't get better if she went to him. He'd stay the way he was. But she couldn't just leave him either.

The washing machine chirped. She pushed herself back, rolling the chair away from her desk. Time to leave the study and get back to work. No time for self-pity. She had to keep living without Chris, everyone agreed to that; she had to be a parent for Ryan. As much as she wanted Chris to come back, she couldn't do nothing while waiting for him to come home. There was Ryan to take care of, keep her fed, sheltered, and moving forward with her life.

Father Green had sent his sister's information and said to meet at a nearby Starbucks tomorrow before lunch. She would probably tell her the same thing all the blogs said: you can't save those who don't want to be saved. Live for Ryan.

May climbed up the stairs toward the laundry room. Had Alicia felt as lost? Did she go about her day, or had she stopped outside her son's door and knocked, hoping to hear his voice.

His door was open. Had it always been?

Chris's sneakers were stacked on top of his Sunday-dress shoes at the foot of his bed.

He had the same sheets for years. Whenever she asked about getting new ones, he'd told her no. He liked the quilted squares running along its edges in that exact pattern no store carried anymore.

May sat down, running her hand along the ridged scar of a seam down the center of the bedspread. It had torn in the wash last winter, and she'd been sure Chris would ask for a new one then, but he hadn't. He had asked for a needle and thread and sewed it back together himself. May had to come back and redo it the next day while he was at school, but that hadn't stopped her from taking them all out to The Egg and I to celebrate his *successful* repair.

As much fun as it was to joke with Chris about buying a new bed cover, she didn't want to get a new one. They'd had it for over a decade. Chris had picked it out at the store himself. He'd been so excited to make the decision for himself; run right up to the display. "This one! This one!"

"That one?" May had asked, other more interesting ones surrounding them. Chris had run past the one with rocket ships as if knowing he'd have this cover long after deciding space exploration wasn't cool anymore—a decision May still hadn't quite gotten over herself.

He'd rolled his eyes at her. "Yeah, Mom."

But she had laughed rather than tell him to stop being a smart-alec. Chris had tried picking up the bedding pack by himself. The whole thing probably weighed as much as he did—it was at least as tall as he was—and he stumbled back a step before half spinning, half hurling the covers into the bottom slot of the cart.

Would he ever make her laugh like that again? Even if he came back, would their relationship ever be that comfortable?

May curled the cover in her hand. If she closed her eyes she could feel the sag of the bed as if he was beside her, reading *Jurassic Park* to himself, but mostly skimming through the science parts to get to the dinosaurs. He'd gasp whenever they came onto the page and read out their description to her. She'd look down toward his captivating smile, pretending to read along with him, but never even glance at the page.

The schoolyard wrapped up around the curving driveway. Groups of kids stood close to the walls, hiding out from the heat in the long shadows. May slowed down and searched for her daughter. She found Ryan standing beside Stacy. The two girls stood side by side, staring at one phone between them, and talking animatedly about whatever was on it. They looked up as May rolled down the window.

"Hi, honey. How was your day?"

"Good," the girls said together.

Stacy reached over and gave Ryan a side-hug. "Text me."

"Hey," Ryan said, climbing into the car. "Can we get Starbucks?"

"Starbucks?" There was one just down the street, but they almost never went there. It must have been a long day at school. Ryan certainly looked stressed: hair tied up in a bun. Lord knew her own day had been long enough.

"Yeah, come on, Mom. It'll be good to get a little treat."

May nodded. It would be good. It almost didn't matter what they would talk about. It would be a distraction, however short it might be. She could spend five minutes without having to worry about what to do: go get Chris, let him find his way home. She could simply be a parent with Ryan.

She could forget about the blogs and the books she'd spent the morning reading, block out all the voices telling her Chris was doomed to Hell, and remember the good times they had before Chris became gay. Before he developed same-sex attraction. That's what everyone called it: same-sex attraction. SSA. Like a virus, an illness or malformation, something wrong, bad, and corrosive. But unlike a virus, Chris chose to have it. He now accepted it; said he was gay.

"I ate lunch with him." Finally, Ryan had said something. She sat back in her seat, arms curled over her waist; another wall between them. "He doesn't want to fight with you."

"He doesn't?"

Surprised, May pulled into a parking space facing the Starbucks with her hands gripping the wheel. She didn't reach over to turn off the engine. Chris didn't want to fight. Why did that make everything seem so much harder?

"No, he . . ." Ryan leaned forward to rest an arm on the center console. She looked miserable: drooping mouth and bags beneath the eyes. "He just wants you to love him."

"I never stopped—"

"I know that. He does too. I know he does, even if he won't say so. But you have to show him you still care. You need to show him it doesn't matter that he's gay."

She shoved the gear into park. "It does matter! It's a sin. You know that. He knows that. Sodomy's wrong. I will never stop loving Chris, but I can't support his lifestyle. Just as I wouldn't support him if he started popping pills."

"It's not—being gay isn't like . . ." Ryan fell back into her seat and groaned.

May sighed and dropped her gaze. Her girl was probably exhausted, all she wanted to do was get Chris back home, same as her. But May couldn't let him live a bad life. Ryan just didn't understand that. It hurt.

Oh honey, it hurt more than anything in the world, but . . .

She took a breath. Chris couldn't come home yet.

"You know," Ryan started again, not yet looking up. "I promised him things would be better if he told you. He thought you'd freak, but I kept telling you wouldn't. Then you go looking into those camps. You know why he hasn't come back yet?"

May scowled. "I'm not sending him away." Lord almighty, she never should have looked into *James Retreat*. Maybe they could have helped, but no one was listening to her anymore.

"Because the two of you are going to fight. If he stays away, he can at least pretend you'd take him back."

"I would!" Her own voice sounded distant. But what a relief to hear someone else say it. It wasn't too late. Her boy could come back. They might fight, but they were still a family, weren't they?

"Even if he came back with *him*?" Ryan said, pointing out the window.

What was *he* doing here? Anthony was sitting at one of the tables outside, one leg crossed over the other's knee as he practically lounged back in the black metal chair. He looked up, glancing around. Something must have—Chris. Her boy was in the Francis school uniform. He'd kept the wrinkled white shirt tucked into the pants, but he didn't look a bit uncomfortable out in the heat. He said something, half-ran, and quickly hugged Anthony. The two parted after a few seconds, but kept their hands clasped together as they disappeared inside.

May released her breath. She hadn't even noticed she was holding it. That was him! Her boy! He looked good, cheeks full and blushed, so he wasn't starving, and he'd run into that hug with a full smile spread across his face.

He was happy, no denying that. Maybe, just maybe, it wouldn't be bad. They could sit down together like they'd done so many times before. Spend the holidays together like a family—Tracy might even come over once. Sit around the Christmas tree, kids all eyeing their gifts, too full from dinner to actually stand and open them. Ryan would be the one to break the over-stuffed spell and begin handing out gifts—pretending to be one of Santa's elves like she always did, skipping from tree to person delivering gifts. Chris and Anthony might help, or they might just stay seated on the couch—they could just sit next to each other. They wouldn't need to hold hands or any-thing. Would that be so bad?

"See?" Ryan asked. "He makes Chris happy. And you know Anthony isn't bad for him. He's nice. You thought so too before you knew they were dating."

Tension fell from her shoulders and her hands relaxed around the wheel. Everything would be simpler if Anthony were a jerk. But he wasn't; he was a good kid. He'd probably be willing to sit down for a talk. Let her explain why a relationship couldn't work between them; that it might be nice for a while, but the boys wouldn't be able to keep it up. They couldn't spend holidays together. They'd never walk hand and hand into a Christmas Mass. They could stay behind with the gifts and the tree or maybe tag along and sit on opposite ends of pews, but in the end it wouldn't matter what they did. They couldn't pretend nothing was different. Because even if she forced herself to look the other way and told herself Anthony was a good kid, nothing would change the fact that homosexuality was wrong. It was a sin: a failing grace. Chris could never take communion. Never receive any of the sacraments.

But without Chris in her life, she couldn't claim to be in a state of grace. Nothing seemed right without him. She needed him home; no matter what everyone said.

"Enough."

"No, Mom. You loved Anthony before you knew he was gay."

"That was before I knew what he was doing to Chris."

"So? They've been dating for months."

"Months?" Why did that word hit like a punch? *Months?* How long of that time had they been lying to her? All that time, pretending the boys were just friends. *Oh God!* How many times had that boy slept over?

"Chris told me after—"

"You're grounded."

"What?"

"You heard me."

"For what?"

"Keeping secrets."

"But. . .." She slumped back into the seat with a half growl.

May ground her teeth; hand tightened around the wheel. Families weren't supposed to lie to each other. They stuck together, through thick and thin, instead of fighting and leaving one another. So what did that make them?

May sat alone, lights off beside a dark computer screen, cradled the phone in her hands, and stared at the front door. Some of her fingers were asleep. How long had she sat here? Why couldn't she just call him already?

He might not even answer. He might not notice or he might ignore it. She should have gone into the Starbucks. Why did Ryan say they'd been dating for months? That had made everything worse. This wasn't just one accident—one slip up in a moment of weakness. It was so much more than a single mistake.

That wasn't going to make the call any easier. After a whole month, he would try and hold even harder onto what he thought he'd found in that boy. He'd probably talk about how happy Anthony made him and she'd need to listen, but at the end, she'd need him to come home.

She'd have to ask, no matter how bad it made her sound, or what she'd have to tell him, or even if it wouldn't fit into their talk at all. She'd have to ask him.

"Chris," she whispered to herself. "I need you to come home."

She gripped the phone tighter in her hands. Yeah, say it just like that. Right up front, ripping out the statement like a Band-Aid.

Come home, sweetie. Just please come home.

The phone shook; its screen lit up with his picture: Chris. She took a deep breath and pushed the button. This was it.

"Chris—"

"What's your problem?" he didn't even say her name. "You can't punish Ryan for not being ignorant. Get on the right side of history and stop being a bitch."

Chapter 12

Call Me Home

BITCH.

Why was that worse than anything she'd read? Because he'd said it. Because it was true. Because he was right; she was a bitch—a failure of a mother.

What kind of mother doesn't run after her son?

May cradled her Starbucks cup and pulled at the protective sleeve so the coffee's warmth seeped around the cardboard. She closed her eyes.

Bitch.

He'd only called her that once before. Hadn't known any better. May had baked some cookies for them and Chris had come running in, nose high in the air, almost pulling his feet off the ground. He'd taken one bite into the still gooey treat, his eyes half closed in that ridiculous, overly-dramatic, kid-ecstasy. "Thanks, bitch." Scott had told him that word at the playground, and he'd come home thinking it meant all the good qualities of a dog: kind and loyal; nice and comforting.

A short burst of air slipped from her nose. She found herself smiling, and her hands tightened around the cup. Damnit. That kind of moment might never happen again.

Jewelry jangled; half a dozen strands of beaded leather swung against a metal disc and cross. A black woman stopped short a few feet away from her. She leaned a little to the side, her tan shawl tilting with her as she peered down toward May.

"Hello?" The woman's curly brown hair flopped across her face and she raised a hand to brush it aside again. "May Flowers, right? I'm Alicia. Father Green's sister."

May started to stand but Alicia waved her back down and unfolded a portable purse hook. The woman didn't seem to mind the silence as she set up the hook and sat down without another word. She smiled then, as if signaling they were about to finally start talking.

"Tully's usually not that great with descriptions, but . . ." she shrugged, bringing both shoulders to almost touch her cheeks.

"Tully?"

"I don't suppose you guys ever call him that, huh?"

"Mostly Father Green."

Alicia chuckled. "Well, I'll let you in on a little Green family secret then. Tully's middle name is Sullivan, but he could never pronounce it right when he was little. Always came out like 'thulliphan'" She had to stick her tongue out a little to get the effect right. "Sorry. Used to telling this story to kindergartners and they love the sound effects. Anyway, he could never say his name right, but he also loved trying to say it. So, our parents started calling him Sullivan, and we started calling him 'thulliphan' but we got tired of spitting on each other, so we shortened it on down to Tully."

"Really?" May forced a smile. Why were they talking about this? They both knew why they were here. No reason to dance around the issue with pleasantries.

"Hand to God, but don't tell him I told you about that. Not until I head back home at least. I still need his couch tonight."

May opened her mouth, but what was she supposed to say to that?

Alicia picked at her finger. "Hmm, yeah. I'm not too funny. Not with adults anyway. Little kids like me well enough, though."

The Cat Empire began playing over the small cafe speakers. Alicia cocked her head to the side, pointing one ear up to the speakers.

"Oh! Is this them? The Cat Empire?"

"This song's 'Sunny Moon,'" May said, nodding.

"Are they really that big of a deal here, or is Tully pulling my chain?"

"They're pretty big. My kids are pretty much groupies for the local cover band."

"Wait, the band's *real*?"

"Yeah." May smiled. There was a concert coming up too. Maybe Alicia could go to the concert and find Chris. He might listen to her. "A group of friends started it a while back and they're good enough to keep getting gigs around town. The city even has them play at the park sometimes. How long are you staying? They're playing this weekend."

"I'm leaving tomorrow night. I need to get back to my kids—students. I don't want them forgetting about me," she laughed. "Or thinking the sub has replaced me."

May nodded along.

Well, there goes that idea.

What was she doing here? She should be back home, working, or researching about same-sex attraction.

"But they'll understand," Alicia went on. "Kids are great like that, you know? Whatever it is you have going on, they'll listen to you and try to make you feel better in their own way. I used to think adults were the same, but then . . . well, I imagine it's about the same for you. Everyone has an opinion about what you should or shouldn't do, but no one really wants to just sit and listen and try to understand what it's like."

She stopped, smiling as she took a breath.

"Tully was actually pretty good about that. He told me he'd be there for Ralph, that's my son, if he wanted to talk, but he needed to be his uncle as well as his priest. I think he understood a little. Enough to know there's nothing like the pain of wanting your son to be happy when you disapprove of the thing that makes him happiest."

"Does it go away?"

"The pain?" she shrugged her shoulders again. "Kind of. It changes. At first, it kept me up at night. Like I had the flu. And I just kept thinking of everything bad that would happen to Ralph if he didn't change. But that went away after a while. Now, I worry if he's safe. You hear things, in the news, you know? And other times, when he talks about his fiancé, I'll feel it start up again. I'll think to myself how much happier he might be with a girl, or of how tradition says he'll go to Hell. On those days it feels more like I'm standing outside in a snowstorm. I know that probably isn't much help, but . . . it changes. That's all I can say about it. It's not something that will go away, but you can forget about it sometimes too."

"The two of you talk?" She had said *talks about his fiancé.* Surely they still talked. Hadn't Ralph left like Chris? Or, was there a way to bring him back?

Alicia took a breath and lowered her gaze. "There was a time when we didn't." She spoke slowly, just like Father Green on the pulpit. "Those were, well, those were hard days, and now it's different than it was before he came out to me."

"What changed? I mean . . ."

"Aside from the obvious?" she smiled; then sighed. "There's a distance now that wasn't there before. He knows I love him, but . . . you're not asking about what's different between us now, are you?"

She paused; rolled her shawl between two fingers. Did she want a response? She shook her head, as if answering.

"He called me one day, about a month after we stopped talking. It was awkward. Nothing like the usual weekly talks we'd been having since he went off to college. It was weird, and forced, and the whole thing ended with him hanging up on me. But I called him back a week later. I hung up on him that time."

Alicia laughed and looked away as she shook her head, a smile plain across her face.

May stiffened. Chris used to make her smile like that.

"We kept in touch after that. The yelling stopped and we started saying I love you to each other again."

The woman held her gaze like it was that simple. And why not? She loved Chris: her infuriating boy who'd hung up the phone and called her names.

"You have to talk. Even if you need to force it. That's the only way you'll be able to keep a relationship with your son."

"What if he doesn't pick up?"

"Then you keep calling. You call him every day until he blocks your number and then if he does that you find out where he's staying and talk to him there. If you want him to be a part of your life, you can't ever give up on him. Let him know nothing will make you stop loving him or leave him alone."

"What if it's too late?"

She laughed again. "It's never too late. Ralph gave me a book once. It talked about the gay character's relationship with his parents. Said there are walls we put up, both us and them, but they don't have to stand forever. It's our choice to let them stand. It's never too late to tear them down."

May kept her hands clutched together in her lap. Her car idled in the shopping center parking lot. Thankfully, only a few cars sat parked beneath the dark green glow of Barnes and Noble's sign and she couldn't see anyone through the storefront windows.

She sighed, had to go in sooner or later. It was almost four; St. Francis had let out half an hour ago, but Ryan wouldn't need to be picked up until five. At least she was doing something. She'd said what it was this morning, but Lord knew what. It was a miracle May had remembered at all.

She clenched her hands, squeezing fingers together as if that small movement would solve anything. Hopefully Alicia's book recommendations would give her some guidance. Or, at least help focus her mind. They could give her something to talk about when she called Chris, act as a peace offering, and show she was trying. If only he would too.

She made the sign of the cross and turned off the ignition. Ryan needed to be picked up soon after all; couldn't wait all day.

Walking towards the store, she pulled out her phone and scanned the list of books. A list of titles appeared in the Notes app. Alicia had said they were written by Christians about their experiences with gay people. Most of the authors weren't gay themselves, but parents of gay kids. She'd promised they were objective and gave facts before moving on to talk about their own experiences.

The Barnes and Noble was about as empty as the parking lot; a few employees walked around or stood behind their registers, but the brown shelves were clear of customers.

May looked up at the green signs hanging from the ceiling. Where would they be? Religion or self-help? Parenting? She scanned the shelves as she walked past. Maybe a book would jump out at her, but there were too many titles to single any out. May turned into the parenting section.

Everybody Poops sat on a pedestal at the far end. A whole set-up surrounded it, as if potty training were the pinnacle of parenting. Books on discipline and autism spread out from that classic. She scanned the labels: diet, schooling, guides to hobbies, then, finally, a shelf dedicated to sex.

Running her fingers along the book spines, she looked for the books. They weren't on this shelf. No, not on that one either. So many books about puberty or safe sex, but nothing on same-sex attraction or having a gay son. Maybe under religion—

"Ms. Flowers."

May froze. She hadn't heard that voice in a long time. She turned and sure enough, a young girl with straight-ironed, platinum-blonde hair stood in the aisle with her. Lisa. She wore khakis and a purple flannel and a name tag hung around her neck. May narrowed her eyes a little. When did she start working here?

"Can I help you find anything?" Lisa smiled, as if they had anything in common after what she'd done to Chris.

"No, Lisa, I'm fine."

May glanced to the shelf. She should have just bought ebook copies.

"There's some more books on the other side." Lisa walked past her and gestured at the other shelf's card: LGBT.

May's face flushed. She shouldn't let anything come in the way of helping Chris. Especially not some girl like Lisa. "Thank you."

"My pleasure." Lisa turned away, swinging her name tag so it lurched in a wide arc. "Just let me know if I can help with anything else," she half sang.

May stared at her. What had her boy ever seen in that girl? She always acted like a child. But she knew where Alicia's books were.

"Wait! Lisa?" The girl stopped, turned around. Maybe she could . . . "How did you . . .?"

"Chris and I talked about it," she sighed. "Some. Before I messed everything up. He kept saying he wasn't gay, but, he never wanted to . . ." she blushed and her eyes fell to the ground. "So I sort of asked him if he liked me that way. And he . . . couldn't answer me. After a time, he said he loved me, but he couldn't love me that way." She shook her head. "I know it's no excuse for what I did, but I do think he's better off without me—with someone he can love, really love. You know?"

No.

Yes.

How could she see things like that? Chris was better off without her, the girl was right on that, but he needed a girl. A wife, kids, family.

"You're not sure, are you? That's why you're here, right?"

Lisa took a halting step toward her; a cautious one, as if unsure if she was helping or making things worse. May wasn't sure of which, herself. She should blame the girl for everything. She was the one who'd cheated, who'd turned Chris off women and thrown him into that boy's arms, but here she was, trying. She could be blamed for everything, but that blame wouldn't be right. Especially if what Lisa said was true. Chris was having those thoughts before she'd cheated. The girl hadn't done anything to help then, but that didn't mean she wasn't trying now.

"I want what's best for him."

"I know." Lisa closed her eyes and took a deep breath. "That's why he waited so long to tell you. It's why he couldn't ever really admit it to me too. He didn't want to hurt us. That's why I did it, you know. I wanted to prove to myself, I guess, that it wasn't me. I didn't make him gay." She played with her name tag, twirling the attached string around her finger like an old phone cord. "And I'm unloading a lot on you, but you should know. It's not your fault."

❖ ❖ ❖

Oh, no . . . of all the times for a traffic jam.

Ryan would have to wait around school a bit longer.

A long line of red brake lights stretched down the road to where a fire truck sat parked, lights flashing, taking up half the stinking intersection. Just going the two blocks would take the better part of an hour. There had to be a way around, but the street was lined with nothing but houses. A low brick wall separated their yards from the road, and a line of trees helped block their view, but the people had to get in and out somehow.

A car ahead turned off the main road, entering the neighborhood. They must have had the same idea she had. May rolled the car forward. She could just cut over one street, then keep heading down the road, hopefully skip the accident.

She flipped on her blinker, turned into the neighborhood, and swore.

Another stupid line of cars. A little plume of dust clouded the end of the street. Construction workers stood around and watched as one drilled into the ground. A detour sign pointed to the right.

May sighed. Hopefully this wouldn't take long. The cars started forward, making their slow turn down the detour path. She turned up the radio; another song started, drowning out the jackhammer with familiar cymbal taps and the bright, rolling chimes of a piano.

You saw the carnival in Rio
You saw them dancing in the sun

She tapped her fingers along the steering wheel, and hummed with the trumpets; short little blasts of sound. "Prophets in the Sky" really was a great song. Smiling, she shook her head. Lord, how was this band so popular? Seemed like hardly a week went by without hearing The Cat Empire somewhere. It wasn't just a rich person thing either; they were big on Rude Street too. Tay had even spray-painted their logo around a few places. It seemed like the band had only gotten more popular. Maybe it was just the kids. They'd been in love with ska ever since that first concert: Fourth of July in Josephine Park. They were all together back then. Henry and Stephanie held Ryan between them; her little arms clutched at both their shirts. Chris and Scott ran in circles through the grass by the Strackes' blanket.

Chris loved to talk about that night. It was one of the few memories he had of Ryan's parents. Ryan always said she remembered it too: dancing in the small space between them, the way the grass pricked at her toes, the music so loud and happy.

May swallowed hard. Chris didn't have any memories of his father like that. Not even half-remembered ones. One time, he'd made a family tree in class; four little drawings with lines connecting them. Chris toward the bottom, a line going straight up to May's feet. Above them towered Henry and Stephanie, and Ryan off to the side, not connected to anybody. They'd stuck that on the fridge for a month—after a long talk and some changes. More lines were added, connecting Ryan so they all formed a big circle.

Maybe that should have been a red flag, a warning that he'd start having same-sex attractions someday. How many of the articles had said homosexuality was caused by a lack of good parents? She'd tried. She'd told him everything about Cesar, answered every question, played his favorite songs, anything and everything to show her boy who his father was.

But what if it wasn't enough?

Chris had promised she was the best mom in the world. But how could that be true? Sons don't leave *great moms*.

Maybe if Cesar had been around, things would have been different.

She took a deep breath. That old chill ran along her arms, and with them the familiar, sad memories. The seeming eternity since he'd been here; the dumb mistakes, high off his head, one after another, that led him to get behind the wheel that night; the excitement he must have felt. *I have a son!*

His ambulance had arrived an hour after she had, but no one had told her—not until after Chris was in her arms and Henry and Stephanie stood by the bed, tears still streaming down their faces even as Stephanie reached out, asked to hold Chris, take him for just a moment. Just one moment. She'd refused. Heart stopping, thudding, breaking. Something was wrong. Cesar wasn't here, hadn't been here for any of it. Her shoulders felt pushed down by realization that he was gone; the air knocked from her lungs. Every part of her was cold except her arms. Chris wriggled in them, little hands pushing against his blanket, wailing.

They didn't need to tell her. In between their sobs of *I'm sorry, I'm sorry, God I'm so sorry,* May had heard herself promising Chris over and over: *It's okay. I've got you, sweetie. Now and forever, now and forever, I've got you. Shhh, shhh, shh.* Her arms had numbly rocked him. *I've got you.*

May gasped and gulped in heavy breaths. The road blurred, vanishing in tear-stained smudges. Trapped in her shuddering chest, her breath burned and trembled. She wiped at one eye. Didn't help much.

What am I doing?

The car lurched upwards. She slammed on the brake and bounced against the seat belt.

Oh Lord! The curb!

Horns blared behind her. She couldn't breathe—her mouth hung open, her heart hammered, air wheezed out but nothing came back in. She doubled over; her forehead slapped the steering wheel and lay against it; her whole body shuddering. Her arms hugged her chest.

Nothing there. Nothing to hold onto, to ground her.

Honk! A loud radio. Pounding blood and ragged breaths; a single question barreled into her mind: *When was the last time she'd held him?* Caught her breath as his little hands clung sleepily around the back of her neck? Or even hugged him—just for the briefest of moments?

They had to do it again.

They would.

She forced her head up. Closed her eyes to stop the tears, even for just one moment.

He would come home.

"Are you okay?"

"I'm going to call Chris tonight." May ignored the question and turned to Ryan, who sat in the front seat this time, long hair hung loose over her shoulders, and scanned her eyes for a reaction. Her girl looked happy; no point in telling her about the curb.

"You are?" Ryan asked, but her eyes didn't grow larger. She didn't look surprised at all: more relieved than anything. As if May were confirming something she'd known all along: everything would be alright. She hadn't needed to break down crying to know that. Funny how it took seeing her little girl to realize that too. The trip to Starbucks and Barnes and Noble had been good, but that little smile promised the call would go well too.

"Can you make sure he answers?" All Chris had to do was pick up the phone. That would be a good enough start.

"Oh, yeah. Sure."

Ryan pulled out her phone. Her fingers danced around the screen for a short, few seconds before she clicked the phone off and looked up.

"He'll pick up."

Why couldn't it be that easy? Send a text, get a response. Call, answer. Come home and be together.

May glanced at the side of the road: the same buildings they passed every day. The same ice cream truck, menu already sun-bleached from a summer outside, sat parked by Exxon; a crowd pressed together despite the heat, inching closer toward their daily treat. Those same flashes of life outside blurred together with the weathered pavement: bright green grass and muted brown brick flashed in between tree shadows, flickering along the windshield like camera shutters. Nothing out there had changed.

The sight of Ryan beside her. An empty seat filled the rearview mirror where her head used to be; pressed up and forward, sometimes slumping back as she laughed or groaned with whatever was being said up front. In those times she would fall back against the seat, grumbling about this or that, always quick to perk back up with a joke, a comment, anything.

Her little girl was silent now. Her head turned away, out toward the window, closed mouth barely reflected in the glass.

This was what they'd come to.

"Mom? Don't yell at him."

May glanced from the road. She'd never been the one to yell at her son; she hadn't called him names.

"Just please," Ryan added, quickly. "Tell him to come home."

"I am—"

"Let me finish. Please, just . . . just listen."

May nodded and Ryan hesitated as if making sure she could go on.

"Tell him to come home, and accept that he's gay. Or thinks he's gay, or whatever you need to do to get him back. Even if you guys have to just forget about all this and each pretend that everything's fine. Because he's right. If you guys fight again . . . that'll be it. He won't come home twice. So just, please, Mom. Forget about everything and tell him to come home."

"I . . ." May's voice caught in her throat. Could it be that simple? He would come home and they would wrap each other up in a hug and be happy.

She sighed. If only it could be that easy. If this were just a matter of picking up the phone, she wouldn't need books. She wouldn't need the advice of online strangers, or priests, concerned friends, anything. She could just pick up the phone.

Chris, sweetie, come home.

But it wasn't easy.

Just saying that wouldn't be enough—it didn't solve anything.

And what would happen next? When he came home he would still think he was gay. Still want to date that boy. Neither of them would talk about it. She'd be too afraid he'd leave again, and he . . . Chris wouldn't mention it either. They'd go back to living together without being a part of the other's life.

Her grip tightened around the wheel. That couldn't happen. Her little boy was going to come home completely; without secrets. She couldn't lie to him and say everything was fine—it wasn't— but they could work through this together.

He just needed to come home.

That's what she'd say. Come home and talk about it like a family. Come home and work through all this together, and never, ever, say *bitch* again.

❖ ❖ ❖

God, let this go well . . .

May sat at her desk, her open hands cradling the thin rectangle of her phone. In a few hours, she'd managed to read one of the books from Barnes and Noble. The rest lay in a slanting pile in front of her. They weren't long, but they didn't need to be. They said being gay wasn't a choice. One of them all but proved it wasn't. The one she'd finished talked about this boy's struggles with coming out. A Baptist kid named Justin who'd spent years trying to be straight, but it never happened. Despite praying, going to counseling, and researching everything he could, nothing changed. He still thought he was gay. It wasn't a choice for Justin. He'd said as much through his entire book.

But that didn't mean there weren't any choices for Chris.

Her boy didn't have to act on his desires. He could have told her about those feelings and ignored them. Found help and support sooner. He didn't need to go behind her back to get with some boy.

She blew the air from her lungs in a slow, controlled stream. Time to call him.

The line rang twice before he answered. "Hello?"

It was him. God, it was him! There was that almost uncertain-sounding greeting he always answered with; the *o* sounding higher than the rest, like a question. When was the last time she'd heard it?

"Chris?"

"Ryan said you wanted to talk."

Lord, his voice was even. Not even a trace of the worry knifing through her chest. He almost sounded happy, as if he was fine staying away.

"Yes," May said. She had to tell him what she needed to. After that . . . after that she'd have to see. "I wanted to call and say . . . say that I love you."

Her voice caught in her throat and she needed to swallow.

No sound came from Chris.

"And I want you to come home."

Her voice cracked. Something knotted in her chest; made her breathing stop and throat burn.

"Please, come home."

Her vision blurred and she brushed the tears out of her eyes. Her throat closed up so tight she probably couldn't say anything without blubbering and crying in earnest.

"Mom . . ." Chris trailed off; a hint of her same pain finally seeping through the phone. "I'm gay. I need to know that it's okay, that you think it's okay for . . . If I come back, that I can come back fully. I can't keep hiding who I am from you."

"Chris—"

"Would you accept Anthony back too?"

Her eyes fell to the books. Buried beneath her new editions was the Bible Henry and Stephanie had given it to her. A note was written on the inside: *To the best mom in the world.* Chris was too young to even know it was Mother's Day, so they'd written it for him. But they'd still sworn up and down it was really from him.

She reached over and placed her hand on the soft faux-leather cover, worn down over the years where her fingers rubbed up against it. She'd promised to always look out for her little boy—give him a better life than she'd had. She couldn't do that if he left again. Had to be honest now. Otherwise, he'd never stay.

"I love you, but I can't—"

"I knew it."

"—see you with him."

"You haven't changed."

"I still love you." Why couldn't that be enough?

A sound wracked through the line: a short, half-choke of a laughing sob. "No you don't."

Click.

"Chris?"

Her hand slipped and fell onto her lap. He wasn't coming home. Why did it have to be this way?

She brushed her eyes, her chest heavy. He wasn't coming home.

She'd have to call again. Every day: again and again until he listened to her. Just like Alicia had said, if she wanted him home, she had to call him.

"Every day." Her breath shook in the whisper.

She would call again tomorrow, and Thursday, and Friday, and every day after that until he came back.

She forced herself to stand; the world spun in a dizzying blackness. He would come back. He would. She just had to call every day, keep the strength to listen to him, and not hang up. No matter what he said, never hang up on him.

Her bracelet slipped downward, its weight against her wrist like the touch of a hand. Somehow she wasn't alone. *Hail Mary, full of Grace . . .* she stopped praying and shut her eyes. Tears welled under closed lids. *Mary? Was it ever this hard for you? Worse, probably. Always worried about who-knows-what kind of mischief he could get up to. Running around with those sheep and other kids, falling down and scraping his knee.* She smiled. *You were probably worried sick. How'd you get through it?*

Goosebumps spread along her arms and a faint chill shivered down her back; just like sitting down in front of her old AC. Tomorrow would go better. All she had to do was call.

She could do this. Call him every day and things would get better.

"Mom?" Ryan's voice echoed from upstairs. There was a thud—her door closing probably, followed by the creak of floorboards. "Is . . .?" Ryan stopped at the top of the stairs. She stared down at May. Her makeup must be smeared. "What did he say?"

May swallowed—no hiding this from Ryan. Her girl deserved to hear what happened. Lord knew she'd find out anyway.

"He asked if I could accept him being gay."

Her eyes widened. "Can you?"

"I don't know."

"What do you mean you don't know?" Ryan folded her arms over her chest.

May tensed, but didn't say anything. She breathed out a sigh instead, letting go of her irritation. Her little girl was tired, same as her. That tone could be ignored for now.

"It's—it's complicated, honey. It's a sin. There's nothing that says otherwise." She gestured toward the stack of books on her desk. Even Justin's book said he could be celibate—he didn't have to date anyone. "But I love him."

Even though he doesn't think so . . .

"I do," she continued. "And nothing he can do will make me stop loving him."

Ryan smiled, but her hands did not relax. They still clenched together against her sides, beneath her armpits.

"But there's more to being a mom than loving him," May continued. "I need to give him the best life he can have, even if that means he'll hate me for a time. I have to raise him right."

"What if you're wrong?"

May turned back to the books, away from Ryan's watering eyes. "I just need him to come home."

Chapter 13

All That Talking

ALICIA WAS PLAYING WITH her shawl again—different from the other day. This one had short strands hanging off. She wrapped them around her finger, curling once before letting them slide out again.

May hesitated in the Starbucks doorway. How long had the woman been sitting like that? No drink, but she stared out at the passing cars. Might have been a few minutes, maybe an hour. There really was no telling how long it had been. The woman glanced over.

"May!" Alicia did not stand, but instead smiled up to her, "How was your night?"

May rested her hand on the back of the chair. She would not, under any circumstances be talking about her little accident. If Ryan hadn't needed to hear about it, Alicia certainly didn't.

"I called Chris." May sat down; Alicia nodded for her to continue. "He hung up on me."

She chuckled; a soft, little laugh. "Kids are all the same, aren't they?"

May stared at her. What was that supposed to mean? Alicia waved her hand, dismissing the comment, so it probably didn't mean much.

"Think he'll call you back?" Alicia asked.

"I don't know."

"Will you?"

Of course! She had to. At least tonight; no excuse not to. She would call him back, he might not answer. But he couldn't hang up on her then.

"Yes."

Alicia smiled, seemingly happy May had made some progress. May couldn't look at that smile. She glanced down. How could this woman be so selfless? She'd spent so much of her trip helping with Chris, and May hadn't done anything in return.

"But what about you?" May asked. "How was your night?"

The simple question wasn't much, but it was something.

"It was pretty good. Tully and I got invited out to dinner by some parishioners, but that was about it. Went to bed pretty quickly. Talked about you and Chris first, of course," she added. "One thing I'll always love about Tully is that he really cares. He's always been that way. Ever since he was little, he always wanted to help people. A lot of the time he couldn't, or didn't know how, but he always wanted to try, and he'd feel terrible whenever he couldn't. That's why he asked me to come, you know. I don't think he could sleep knowing the trouble you and Chris were having."

"He asked you to come?"

"I would have come anyway if I knew you myself. Like I said yesterday, the worst part of all this is not having someone to talk with."

May looked down at the table. What was she supposed to say to that? *Thank you?* No way those words could repay Alicia for what she had done. No small talk could show enough gratitude, but there wasn't anything else to say.

"Thank you."

"Oh, my pleasure. I know talking with me must be wonderful," she laughed, as if her help were that simple. "Not that I'm that great or anything, but . . "

"Anything helps," May agreed. She would have been so lost without her talks; however short they'd been. She'd really have to do something for her before leaving.

She smiled. "Well, now, I'd like to think I'm better than just anything."

"You are! You are. Those books were a great recommendation."

"So, what do you think?"

"I'm not sure it's a choice." She had to say everything right so she could repeat it when she called Chris tonight. "Not the attraction at least. I think, being attracted to other men, that may be a cross for him to bear. But I still don't think it's right. He shouldn't . . . date men. There, I don't see a choice between right and wrong. It's just wrong."

"Why do you think that?"

The way Alicia asked it didn't seem accusatory or directed at her; just asking her to say more. She was like her brother that way, inviting May to explain her belief.

"Sex is for marriage. Anything more is just for your own pleasure. It's lust."

"What if he and Anthony were married?"

May hesitated. Would that be okay? No, that wouldn't change anything. Married or not, they were still two men and marriage was meant to be something more.

She shook her head. "Two men can't have the gifts of the Holy Spirit."

"What if they promised to be chaste in their vows?"

"So what? They'd just be friends?"

She chuckled again. "Really close friends, but yes. They'd get married for legal rights in this case."

"If that were the case, I don't think it would be a sin for them to be friends like that, but that isn't a marriage is it?"

Where was Alicia going with this?

"Is marriage just sex then?"

"No. No, there's more to it than that, so I guess they could get married—as friends. If they're abstinent."

"But what if they had sex sometimes?"

May crossed her arms. That went right back to where they started. The sex was the sin. Didn't she understand that? Or was Alicia trying to say something else? Was she making fun of her?

She shook her head. No, that wouldn't work. "That'd be his choice."

"But it's our choice too."

May stared at Alicia. That didn't make sense.

"What do you mean?"

She was smiling, but her smile was relaxed. Calm. Whatever this was, it wasn't meant as a trick.

"It's our choice—how we view them. How we treat them. I don't think the sin matters as much as the rest. Looking at it, it's the sex that we're looking at here not their love for one another. Now maybe this makes me a bad Catholic, but I don't really care what tradition says about sex. At least, I don't think it matters so much on this issue compared to everything else. What matters is loving them. And I mean real love. Not that 'Love the sinner, hate the sin' stuff, because all that is is love at arm's length. Trust me, I loved Ralph that way for a long time."

Alicia closed her eyes. She took a breath, shoulders rising as she held it.

"And Jesus said a lot about love. It's the most important thing, the Great Commandment: love. Matthew, Mark, Luke, and John. Even Paul! They all agree about love."

"It's not that simple—"

"Isn't it? Love is what brought your family together. It's what kept mine together, and it's what brought me down here. It's what'll bring Chris home too."

"What if it's wrong?" she wanted to shout the question, but heard it like a whisper. "What if he doesn't go to Heaven?"

Alicia stared at her, gaze softening as her mouth turned to a pitying half-smile. "Oh, May . . ." She reached over the table to rest on hand atop May's. "I don't think we have a say in that. Not really. That's between them and God Almighty. We teach them right, but it's up to them to follow those morals. If they choose wrong—if being gay is wrong . . ." She pulled her hand back. "Then, it's wrong. But that doesn't mean we do what's wrong too."

On the spot where Alicia had touched: a soft tingle began. She had said it like it was so easy: do the right thing. But what was the right thing? She said love. Love above everything. Maybe that was it; a simple, impossibly hard fix. Or maybe she was wrong and it wouldn't work out. No way of knowing now, but one thing was for sure. She had to try. And Chris had to come home.

May turned into the driveway. Elizabeth's house loomed just a few hundred feet away. Her stomach coiled in on itself and she bit her tongue. Funny how things went so bad so quickly.

It wasn't always that bad, though. Sometimes relationships just drifted apart and other times they just vanished.

If things go badly with Chris, how will they go? One big fight like the one Ryan's afraid of and that's it? Or hundreds of unanswered calls and small let downs?

May took a breath and turned off the car. It didn't have to be that way. Alicia was right about that. Walls get built up, bridges get burned or fall apart, but it's never too late to make amends. Funny, too, how Alicia had only been around a few days, but was already doling out life advice like they grew up together. They'd only talked for an hour or so all told, but they had that shared connection of their kids. Would that connection last past this week?

It would be sad if it didn't. After everything, the girl should know how helpful she'd been. Even if . . . even if she didn't have good news to tell her.

May looked back to Elizabeth's house. There were a lot of people she should talk to.

She pulled out her phone and typed in the old number as her fingers drummed along her leg. What if someone else answered? Or what if there wasn't an answer? Where would she even start with the message?

The ringing stopped.

May squeezed her eyes shut. She could barely get out a word. "Hello?"

"I swear to God, if you're another one of those robo-callers—"

"Tay?"

Tay didn't say anything back. Maybe it wasn't her. Maybe she got a new landline or moved or disconnected it and someone else got the number. Who knew who was on the other end? She should just apologize and hang up. This was dumb. Just another bad call in a long line of failed attempts to—

"Mayflower! Is that you? How you doing, girl?"

She hadn't been called that name in years. May laughed and it came out almost like a snort the way she'd laughed back in grade school. It was her! Oh, Lord! What a wonderful thing to her Tay's voice again.

May stood in Ryan's doorway. Her little girl sat cross-legged on the bed, forgotten textbook illuminated by the down-turned shine of her phone's bright screen.

May leaned against the open door and held her breath. Should she go in? Or, not. Apologize first, and then see about coming in.

"I shouldn't have grounded you. You were just doing what you thought was right, and . . . well, I'm sorry, honey."

"It's alright." Ryan nodded a little, but didn't say anything else.

May hesitated, one foot in the room—too much to say. Alicia had left her at Starbucks with a final word of encouragement, and just like that she had gone, leaving May alone to repair her family. Ryan was just the first step; also the easiest. The girl could never hold a grudge against anyone; she was like her mother in that way. Nice to everyone, even to those who didn't deserve forgiveness.

"Dinner will be at seven."

She meekly backed out the door. If only talking with Chris could go so well.

As she walked past his room, Ryan shut her own door. May stopped and slipped her hand around the doorknob. The cold metal turned in her hand, twisting the knob slowly so it wouldn't squeak and pop. She took a deep breath then leaned against the door, silently gliding the door open as if he was asleep inside and she was just checking up on him.

Light poured through the blinds, caught and bounced off the floating dust. Nothing had changed. She hadn't been back since closing the door . . . two days ago? Was that all?

She slipped into the room and eased the door shut. His room hadn't changed in years. The same posters of The Cat Empire hung on the wall from middle school. The desk was crowded with the same collection of books and stack of newspaper comic strips he'd carefully cut out. He'd always promised he would find a place for them, but he could never decide which ones he actually wanted to preserve in a booklet.

He hadn't shown her one in years. How long ago had he started collecting them? Fifth grade, at least. It all started with a class project—read the newspaper for a week—and after that he got hooked. He'd skim the Arts & Culinary sections, but the comics were his favorite. So May had always saved the whole paper for him just in case he ever wanted to look at the rest. He'd run to the kitchen table and read through it—his face a mask of complete seriousness, as if reading the actual news. But then he'd come across one that made him laugh and his whole face would light up. He'd keep smiling too until he cut out his new favorite strip and stored it with the others.

She pulled out her phone, holding it to her ear as it dialed, then rang, and went to voicemail.

May dropped the phone from her ear. He hadn't answered. The faint voice asked her to please record a message. She had to talk. Even if he wasn't going to listen to it.

"Chris, this is Mom. I was just, just calling to let you know that I . . . I want . . . I talked with Father Green's sister today. She has a gay son too, and well . . ." she had to swallow. Something lodged in her throat. She forced it down and took a deep breath; her throat on fire. "I want you in my life again, Chris. I want to be a part of your life, too. I don't like not talking with you, no matter how hard it is, or how often we say the wrong thing. I—I just need to be a part of your life again. Please, call me back when . . ." Her voice caught and scratched at her throat. She couldn't do this. "Can we meet somewhere? I can't do this over . . . I need to see you, Chris." Her throat was raw, but she couldn't hang up. She had to tell him first, even if he wouldn't listen to her, she had to say it: "I love you."

She lowered the phone and hung up with a sigh. Would he call back? Her folded hands traced around the beads on her bracelet, but she didn't say anything. No prayers came, not ones with words anyway. Sitting there, it was easy to forget, to pretend to forget, to pretend it was possible to forget this last week. She could sit and be waiting for Chris to run upstairs from the kitchen; scissors in hand as if she hadn't told him just yesterday to not run with them. But he was always too excited to listen. Small hands would shove a carefully cut piece of newspaper into her hand, and she would laugh at whatever it said.

She looked around the room again. Why couldn't things go back to the way they were?

Her phone buzzed: Chris.

Does after school Friday work?

Five-thirty, only half an hour until her boy's first track event. First sporting event ever really. May reached for the ignition and released her breath. If Ryan noticed her nervousness she didn't let on. She still leaned forward, hands practically on the dashboard as she stared at St. Francis's small stadium. Father Green had gone all out today.

He must really be serious about that sports ministry program of his.

Two booths were set up by the front entrance, selling all sorts of baked goods and drinks as a handful of dads grilled hamburgers and hot dogs behind them. Just inside the stadium's small chain-link fence towered a giant, castle-shaped bounce house. The blue-and-gray walls rocked side to side as screaming kids threw themselves at every inflated surface. A crowd of people milled about in small circles leading to the stands. A whole bunch of kids, but none of them Chris.

May climbed out of the car and scanned the crowd again. Still couldn't see him. She let out another breath, shoulders relaxing.

She swallowed. What type of mother felt good about that? But what would she say? Being gay wasn't right, there was just no way to ignore it. Alicia wasn't right about that part. There had to be more for Chris than just love him and ignore everything else. They'd have to confront this issue. No matter how uncomfortable it might make them, they would have to talk about it. Otherwise, what was the point? Alicia was right when she'd said loving at arm's length wasn't love at all—but was it love to not want what's best for someone else?

Ryan stopped a few steps ahead and glanced behind her, as if checking to make sure May was following. "I think Chris is with the other runners."

May nodded. No need to disturb him before the race anyway. There'd be time to see him after. Maybe then she'd know what to say.

They headed into the stadium, but didn't even slow down at the snack tables. May's stomach churned with each step. She rubbed sweaty hands against her jeans. Her sweetie was here somewhere.

He might be on the other side of the football field. The track circled around the grassy field, and on the other side a group of kids stood in the endzone. White bibs pulled at their shirts and fluttered in hands as the kids pinned the papers onto one another.

He must be there. Maybe towards the back, behind some of the taller kids.

"Alright, alright, alright," a poor Matthew McConaughey impression blared out across the stands. "Who's ready for St. Francis's first track meet?"

The question sputtered and crackled; a speaker hung from a light post. A few people clapped.

"Okay, yes! Now, give it up for our first runners!"

"That's the kindergarteners, right?" Ryan asked. "Can they even run at that age?"

May pulled her gaze away from the endzone and laughed. Her little girl must be trying to make her feel better. Were the nerves that obvious?

"They're not that young. About six years old."

"Still though . . ."

May looked back to the field. Father Green walked across the grass, leading a group of small kids toward the track. She scanned the other runners, looking for any sight of her boy, but Chris still wasn't anywhere.

The first group was a mix of younger kids: probably kindergarten to first or second grade. A handful of the kids were a good half a foot taller than the rest. Father Green lined them up at the start of the track's straightaway. Some bent down into a low crouch, others just stood and looked over at the crowd, but all of them fidgeted and squirmed as they waited for the race to start. Two volunteers pulled tight a bright red ribbon across the other end of the track. The kids must only be running the first stretch.

Chris hadn't mentioned that. Maybe it was just for the little kids. But then again, they hadn't been talking much, had they? He'd been pulling away for months, but everything had felt right until that night.

Father Green started the race, swiping his hand down through the air. The kids took off running and parents cheered. May smiled as the kids awkwardly stumbled into the run. It was so much simpler when he was little. The biggest mistake he'd make back then was running with scissors, and there weren't ever any questions about that. It was just something that shouldn't be done.

May looked over to the crowd of other runners. Some had crept closer to the track, but her boy wasn't one of them.

Scattered applause. Ryan nudged her. The race was finished? Already?

Father Green announced the winner as the next group of young kids ambled to the track. Still no Chris. Maybe he was sitting down behind the crowd. He wouldn't miss the event, would he? He couldn't be that mad at her. He'd spent months training for this.

She held her breath. No. He was probably just stretching. A wall of kids blocked off her sight to the ground behind them. That had to be it; she couldn't have ruined this for him. He'd be here.

May forced herself to look away from the endzone. If she kept staring at them, she'd worry herself to death. Another group of kids had started running. Two of the oldest-looking kids broke into the lead immediately. Two girls, wearing matching red shorts and shirts, were neck and neck.

"Go, Jill!" someone shouted behind them. Must be one of the girls' parents. "Jill! Jill! Jill!"

One of the girls pushed ahead of the other and the parents exploded into cheers behind her. The other girl ducked her head and closed the gap, coming back so they were side by side. The volunteers held the flimsy ribbon firm as the girls tore through it. All the cheers stopped at once. Who won?

Father Green looked uncertainly at the volunteers who returned the look with their own of panic before shrugging.

"It's a tie!" Father Green shouted.

The whole stand broke into applause as both girls held hands and raised them in triumph.

Another group lined up. This one went to the traditional staggered starting line, so they'd probably be running the full length of the track. These kids looked like middle-schoolers. Some tall and lanky, others just starting to hit their growth spurts. Lord, how many pants had she bought for Chris? He'd just kept on growing.

Father Green raised his hand to start the race. The crowd took a breath together, as if getting ready to scream all at once for their kids. He dropped his hand, the race started, and Elizabeth walked in front of them.

Everyone else erupted into cheers as the woman stared down at her.

"May."

The woman said it just like the better mom she thought she was.

"Elizabeth."

Matt seemed to appear out of nowhere behind his wife, shifting his weight from one foot to the other. Clearly, he didn't want to be in this situation. He must have known what had happened, and probably heard a whole bunch of lies alongside the truth too.

"Good to see you, Matt."

May smiled. She could be pleasant to him. There was nothing to say to *her* though.

"Excuse me," Jill's mom asked. "Can you take a seat?"

Elizabeth looked up at the woman.

"I was just leaving," she huffed, as if that made her exit any less of a retreat.

Matt raised his hand in a little half wave as he passed by. Maybe he didn't agree with Elizabeth. She should call him after everything with Chris was taken care of. Maybe they could still be friends. This was all Elizabeth's fault—if she'd been a better friend . . . maybe things would have gone differently. Better at least. She wouldn't have been so alone before Alicia showed up.

May stopped herself from cursing, mumbling her frustrations instead. Ryan glanced over at her, eyebrows raised a tad as if she could hear her. She didn't say anything, but she didn't need to. That slight look said everything. May shouldn't be hiding curses in public. They had to fix this and get Chris home.

The parents around her applauded and the rest of the kids started across the field. No one left in the endzone. Chris had to be somewhere in this group; most were familiar faces from St. Francis. There was Scott. He walked along the edge of the group, but still no Chris. How hard was it to find—?

Her chest clenched and missed a beat. Those long arms hung tight against his sides—Chris! Her back stiffened and she tried to push herself up to see higher, get a glimpse of more of her boy. Chris walked beside Anthony; far enough apart that she'd think they were just friends if she didn't know any better.

They lined up on the track, and Father Green raised his hand. May's heart thudded back into her chest, anxiously pounding. Her boy was about to run! God, just please don't let him trip. Or come in last. A respectable run was all he needed.

The hand dropped, and her boy took off running. He passed a few boys in seconds and was close to the front by the first turn. Lord, he was fast!

"Wooo! Chris!" Ryan shouted.

The boys started on the straightaway; her own Chris within a stride of the lead. Forget a respectable run—he could win this! Only a few kids left. He gained on one boy as they entered the final turn.

Cheers broke out behind her and the stands vibrated beneath her feet. Some people even stood up as the runners entered the last stretch, Chris just half a step behind. He could do this!

The red ribbon pulled tight and a chest pushed through, stretching the fabric and tearing it across the middle. May leapt to her feet. Her boy crossed the finish line not a second later, the ribbon still fluttering in the air. She cheered, voice cracking, losing her voice, and screaming her head off.

Third place!

Only two people had finished before him—Anthony and the winner.

Her boy'd placed in his first-ever track event!

As Father Green announced the winner's name and the crowd cheered again, Anthony ran over and lifted Chris up into a hug, spinning him, and shouting something drowned out by the applause.

He turned to her, their gazes locked, and his eyes seemed to glow: tears glistened, illuminated by the fading sunlight. An old breeze flushed down her back; cold AC, driving with windows down, Chris. Her sweetie was right there!

She started cheering again. Hands pounding together, not caring who turned to stare. Her boy was right there! And he couldn't help but see how proud she was of him.

Chapter 14

Won't Be Afraid

"GIVE IT UP FOR our runners!" Father Green's voice echoed across the stands.

The other parents clapped and stomped their feet, cheering for their own kids louder and louder until the applause shook the stands.

Twenty yards away, Chris stood halfway on and off the track; rocking back and forth slightly, leaning ever-so-slightly toward Anthony. Left hand wrapped around his wrist, head bowed low, Chris stared down at the edge of the track, as if wanting nothing more than to run away.

She blinked back tears, hands no longer clapping. That's what would happen. As soon as Father Green stopped talking, her boy would leave.

"Thank you all for coming."

Oh, God. This was it. The cheers stopped: race over.

Chris turned and stepped off the track. He slipped past Anthony. The boy reached out to grab his hand, but Chris pulled free; hardly even stopping.

He couldn't just leave.

May threw herself down the stairs, standing in the front walkway before Chris could take another step. She grabbed the end-rail and leaned over the cold metal.

Father Green glanced up at her, not seeming to notice Chris leaving behind him. He raised his eyebrows, as if asking what was wrong, but didn't stop talking. Something about food.

May's hands slid along the cold metal rail. She had to stop him—show him that she still loved him, was proud of him. Sure, he thought that he was gay, but he'd done so much. He'd come in third tonight. First track event, and he'd already medaled!

She ran from the stands. Chris headed toward the fence-gate; almost at the field's edge and . . . was he dragging Anthony behind him? Were they playing, or no? The boy pulled at his hand and glanced around, as if searching for something. His eyes locked onto hers.

Anthony grabbed Chris by the shoulders and her boy finally turned toward her. May froze, reached out, and clenched the waist-high fence between them. That stupid fence in the way. His cheeks were pale and covered in sweat. Probably exhausted from running so fast.

May took a breath and shook herself out of the moment. He'd done so well. They should go out and celebrate. The thought sent a cold rush through her. That's what they would have normally done. She'd reach out and hug him, tell him how proud she was, and then they'd all go out to eat, and everything would be perfect. They could still do that. Even if . . .

May let out a shaky breath. . .

. . . even if he wouldn't come home.

Even then, he should know how proud she was. She could tell him that. Have one last bit of normal.

Chris scowled. "See? Look at her stare. Nothing's changed."

Chris gestured toward her, a small motion that brought her out of her daze. Her hands still clutched the chain-link fence. She couldn't let go, open her mouth, do anything that would make him leave again.

"Give her a break." Anthony smiled when he spoke—Chris was looking at him—but when they both turned to her that smile disappeared. He glanced down at her whitening knuckles and stared.

May pulled her hands back; the chain-link snapping back against the supporting bar. She took a shuddering breath. Remember what Alicia said. *If you want Chris in your life, you have to reach out to him. Every single time you can. Otherwise . . .*

Otherwise there wouldn't be anyone to blame but herself.

"Well?" Chris crossed his arms. He set his jaw, but didn't look at her; instead, he glanced back toward the people trickling out of the stands.

"I missed you."

Chris turned to her—looked her in the face for the first time in too many days. His mouth twitched. First curling up, then relaxing, mouth opening to hang loose. It only took a moment, she could have imagined it, but her heart clenched in her chest. He didn't say anything more. Just stood there. Maybe waiting for her to say something more.

Her chest hurt too much to speak. Where to begin?

Anthony nudged Chris.

"Me too."

Her heart unclenched. She released her breath, but still couldn't speak.

They fell silent again, the kind of awkward, heavy silences happy families noticed, talked about in hushed tones and subtle tilts of the head. One of those weird silences with everything to say and no way of saying anything. A hundred questions filled her mind, any of which could start up their conversation. But all those questions led to the same place. One of them would get mad and leave, or one of them would say something they could never take back. They would part ways and that would be it.

If nobody spoke, then the silence could last forever. They could make this moment go on and on. Just wait by this fence until night, then morning.

"I'm going to get a hot dog," Anthony said. He looked back and forth between them. "Can I get you anything?"

Chris shook his head, but Anthony didn't leave. He waited, looking at her—wanting an answer.

"No." She couldn't keep anything down.

Anthony nodded and turned back to Chris, giving him a look, the kind any parent gives their kids. The look said one simple word: behave.

He stepped away from them, glancing over Chris's shoulder to her. Surely, he must want them to talk and end the tension between them. The boy had left them alone for a reason; that look of his had made that clear enough.

"You were fast." Her voice sounded soft, almost like a whisper, as if she couldn't speak properly. But she had to try.

"Thanks." He smiled, the first real connection between them all week.

"Those morning runs seem to have paid off."

"Yeah, I'm really glad I started . . ." His smile widened, then seemed to collapse into itself. His gaze fell onto that fence between them, but it didn't stay there long. He glanced up again as if checking for a reaction. "More people here than I expected."

Running was a dangerous topic, apparently.

"Father Green was hoping for more non-St. Francis people."

"There'll be more next time."

May scanned the crowd, looking for any completely unfamiliar faces—most of the people here were from the school. Ryan was back at the stands, talking with Stacy, and . . . May swallowed—oh, no. Anthony stepped forward. He stopped off to the side, balancing two hot dogs and a cup.

Chris followed her gaze. Anthony glanced away, as if he could pretend he hadn't been watching and waiting for them to talk by themselves. But Chris waved him over, apparently not wanting time alone, and Anthony started towards them.

"I got you an Arnold Palmer." Anthony held the cup out to her.

May didn't reach for the cup, freezing in place instead. He'd remembered her favorite drink. She didn't even remember telling him about it. And for that matter, how'd he even find one? Probably had to ask for it special. The boy was thoughtful to do that. He really was a nice boy—cared about others, but he was gay. If only that wasn't so important. If only his thoughtfulness, his optimism and compassion could be everything. But it wasn't.

Why did *that* have to be so important?

"Thanks," she mumbled, finally took the drink, and their smiles were gone.

Maybe it was the way she said that or the awkward handoff of the drink, but the moment passed. Anthony stayed on her side of the fence, but leaned up against it and slipped his arm over the metal to stroke Chris's hand. The boy might as well have jumped over the fence to hug Chris.

"So, what were you talking about?" Anthony asked in that awkward lilt of someone trying to rekindle a conversation.

Neither of them answered. May looked away. Would it always be like this? God, please no.

"The race," she said. "You boys were great."

"Oh, yeah?" Anthony laughed and it only sounded half-forced this time. "We should've won though. Who was it that got first?"

"Caleb," Chris said.

"Yeah, him. He started early. Such a cheater . . ."

Anthony kept his easy grin and they went back to silence. A family walked past them, staring as the three of them just stood there, looking at one another. May watched Anthony's easy grin.

"Look, you should talk about it," Anthony broke the silence again.

God, please no. Just a few more minutes together.

"Let's talk about school first," May said.

"So you can pretend I'm not gay?"

"Yes." Her whisper fell like a building. A huge weighted lifted with that one breath. But her whisper seemed to surprise them. Why? What surprised them more? That she told them or that she felt that way?

"You—"

"I just want things back the way they were."

"—can't actually think—"

Anthony put his hand on Chris's shoulder, silencing him before he could continue.

"I don't want you to be . . ." She smiled, making a small hiccupping noise as a laugh stuck in her raw throat. "I sit in your room when Ryan's not home, and I'll close my eyes and pray that when I open them you'll be there with me, but it won't be you. It'll be you as a kid, hardly a year into school, laying on your stomach with math so simple even I can help you with it."

She took a shaky breath; sore throat burned, hot tears scorched her blurry vision. "I don't . . . I can't . . . I can't stand the thought of you going to Hell. But I can't bear to live without you. God! I don't know anything right now . . . except I'd do anything to get that little boy back."

"Mom . . . that's impossible."

"I know, but I still want you back. I want you back in my life. I can't lose you. Not to . . ."

"Not to *him*? Jesus!" Chris slapped his hand on the chain link fence, rattling the metal. "Mom, I'm gay!"

His eyes went wide. He looked around, slouching as if he could hide on the field. Wheeling around, he stormed away without turning back.

May's face tingled, her arms slumped loose at her sides. *No.*

"Chris!" Anthony called as he jumped over the fence. He shouted the name again, running after him.

She couldn't breathe. Her throat was on fire. She couldn't even open her mouth to cry.

Oh God.

Go after him.

Chase him down!

Her thoughts yelled at her, but she couldn't move. Her boy was leaving her again. Maybe forever. The idea clawed her heart, squeezed her chest, filling her mouth with bile. She'd tried, and he'd ignored her. Left!

Make him see you care.

Don't let him leave.

Something touched her, a soft weight, ahand on her shoulder. "Is everything okay?"

May shrugged off the hand and ran along the fence. The world tilted and whirled beneath her feet. She held onto the fence, supporting her stumbling with the cold metal barbs. "Chris!"

Anthony caught up with Chris, grabbed his arm, and pulled him to a stop.

"The two of you need to talk," he said, glaring between the two of them. "The way I see it, the only thing stopping you is yourselves."

"No, it's her ignorance."

"Call it what you want, I don't like it. I don't—"

"So you're—"

"Let her talk," Anthony ordered.

Chris's mouth snapped shut and May swallowed. The knot remained lodged in her throat. She swallowed again, trying to force down her tears. This was it.

"I don't want to lose you. For the first time in a long time I don't know what to do, and I've read a dozen books since . . . since I saw the two of you. And the one thing I've learned is there's no simple answer here. A lot of people say it's a choice—but I don't believe that. I don't think you'd choose to rebel like this. But being gay doesn't mean you have to act on that impulse."

"So we should be celibate?"

"I don't know." The whisper took all her breath. Her lungs strained like she'd been trapped underwater.

"You can't seriously think—"

"Please, Chris." May wiped at her eyes; blurring her son's image into a smudgy double that spun and shook along with her quaking legs. "Please, let me finish. After that, you can say whatever you want; tell me what a horrible mother I've been, how I never should've looked at that camp, how I should have run after you the moment the door closed—and you'll be right. Because it was me who made you run away. Not God or biology or anything else. I'm the one who threw my own son out onto the streets."

"Mom . . ." The world came back into focus—he came back into focus. The smallest things she'd missed jumped out like lightning in a storm: brown eyes so full of life even now, tinged with red.

Anthony let go of Chris's hand.

"That was *my* choice and I have to live with that. If being gay's a choice doesn't matter. I chose to do that to you. I chose to put you out because I was afraid of what would happen if I didn't. I was scared of something that makes my skin crawl. I still am and nothing that any of those books I've read will change that. I still don't think it's right, but . . . but I could be wrong. I don't know. All I know is that I love you. We can figure out the rest. I don't think what you two do is right, but then again our whole family isn't quite right. But I know God's forgiven my sins every time I see your smile."

She took a deep breath; held the air in her chest so her heart pounded loud against her lungs.

"At the end of the day, that smile of yours is what matters. You're the greatest gift God ever gave me, and I love you. And I'm going to love you no matter what. And I'll try, Chris, I'll try with the people in your life. But I'm going to fail at that sometimes and I'm going to need you to forgive me when I do."

She closed her eyes and lowered her head. Her chest heaved, and her heart pounded back against a surge of sobs. What would he say next? Maybe it wasn't enough? He was leaving her. He didn't love her. She had messed it all up. She was going to lose him, never speak to him again after today.

His arms wrapped around her, squeezing against her sides. His head fell against her shoulder and he exhaled, pushing against the crook of her neck. He pulled her close and didn't say a thing.